The pounding increased—both at Steve's front door and in his head.

With a vicious oath he swung his long legs off the bed and stumbled over his jeans. He debated pulling on the pants. Then he looked down. If the miserable excuse for a human being at his front door had the nerve to wake him, he could take him as he was. Butt naked.

He flung open the door, a blistering comment on his lips. He never uttered it. The sobbing woman on his doorstep thrust a blanketed bundle at him and backed away.

"Hey! Wait a minute! Where are you going?"

A look of terror flashed across her features and she fled down the hall.

"Get back here!" Steve yelled.

And then the baby began to cry.

Dear Reader,

As any parent will tell you, it's amazing what havoc one tiny baby can wreak. But when it's a mystery baby left on your doorstep by a hysterical woman on the run, you can imagine what's in store!

So begins *Mystery Baby* by newcomer Dani Sinclair. It's the first book in the LOST & FOUND trilogy. In each book you'll follow one mystery baby or another's tiny footsteps through a maze of intrigue. Don't miss the continuing stories: *The Baby Exchange* by Kelsey Roberts and *A Stranger's Baby* by Susan Kearney.

Look for all the LOST & FOUND titles in the next two months.

Regards,

Debra Matteucci
Senior Editor & Editorial Coordinator
Harlequin Books
300 East 42nd Street
New York, New York 10017

Mystery Baby

Dani Sinclair

Harlequin Books

TORONTO • NEW YORK • LONDON
AMSTERDAM • PARIS • SYDNEY • HAMBURG
STOCKHOLM • ATHENS • TOKYO • MILAN
MADRID • WARSAW • BUDAPEST • AUCKLAND

This book is dedicated to Barbara Ann Hein, sister, best friend, toughest critic. And to Roger, Chip and Dan. I wouldn't have succeeded without you.

Special thanks to Elaine McSchulskis, Beth Harbison and Jacki Frank. And to an extraordinary friend, Rhonda Harding-Pollero, talented author, fantastic mentor, goddess extraordinaire.

ISBN 0-373-22371-4

MYSTERY BABY

This edition published by arrangement with Harlequin Books S.A.

Printed in U.S.A.

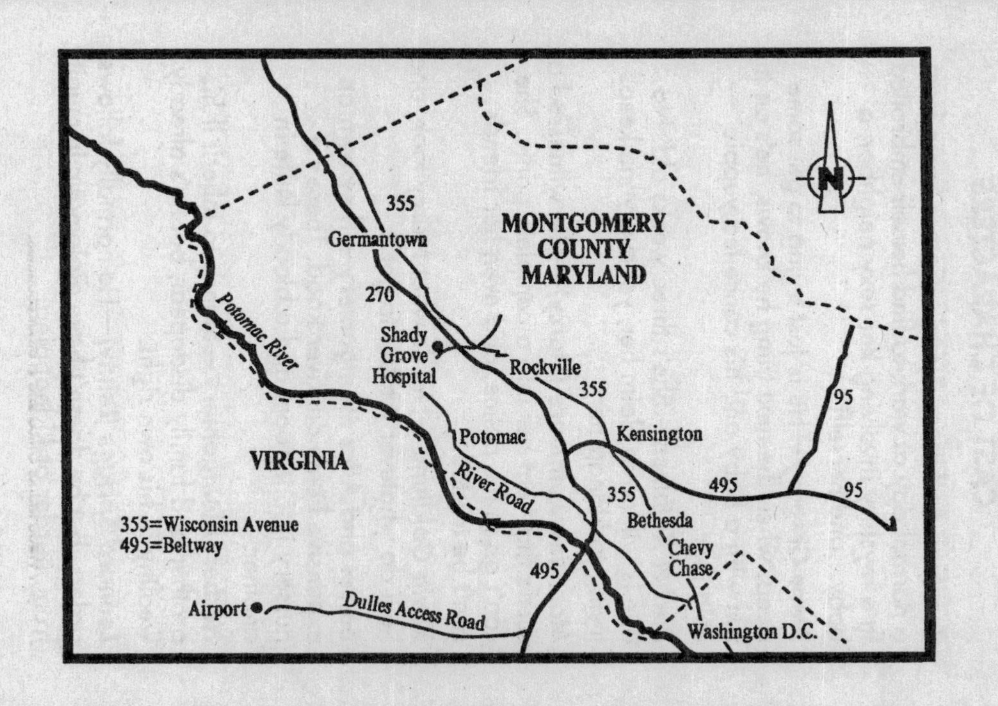
N
MONTGOMERY
COUNTY
MARYLAND
355
Germantown
270
Shady
Grove
Hospital
Rockville
355
95
Potomac
Kensington
VIRGINIA
Potomac River
River Road
495
95
355
Bethesda
Chevy
Chase
495
355=Wisconsin Avenue
495=Beltway
Airport
Dulles Access Road
Washington D.C.

CAST OF CHARACTERS

Jerrilynn Rothmore (Lynn)—Comes home from a normal day at work to find herself embroiled in a mystery involving her sexy neighbor, a baby...and herself!

Steve Gregory—He is just trying to get some sleep, when the next thing he knows, he's on the run with a baby and his conceited yuppie neighbor.

Rachel Kathleen—She's three weeks old. No one is willing to claim her, yet everyone keeps trying to kidnap her.

Marcilina Rothmore (Marcy)—She witnessed a scene that sent her into a complete panic. She can't go to the police, and even her friends can't be trusted.

Kevin Goldlund—Needs what Marcy took, and he'll do whatever it takes to get it.

Barret and Alice Montgomery—They own an expensive home on River Road. There's a nursery in one room and a bloody knife in another.

Herbert Montgomery—Stands to inherit if his brother and family disappear, but he's already wealthy in his own right.

Leonard Spriggs (Lenny)—He normally follows orders, but he doesn't have diplomatic immunity from murder or kidnapping.

Chapter One

A silent scream climbed her throat. Frozen by a terror so gripping she couldn't move, she watched as something flew from the struggling woman's hand to clatter against the stove and slide to the far corner of the room. The man released her and the woman fell back. Her head smacked the counter and in one continuous motion, she slid to the floor and stopped moving altogether. Everyone stopped moving. The two well-dressed men stood there, panting hard.

"Bloody hell," one whispered softly, his British accent easily identifiable. "I think you killed her."

"No."

But he watched, his face stark with fear, as the other man bent quickly over the woman. He ran shaking fingers through his thinning red hair. "She cut me." He pulled back his suit coat to reveal a long gash that stained his white shirt a brilliant red.

"Why didn't you grab the knife?"

"I didn't even see the bloody knife," the other protested. "I thought you said it was under control. I thought you said this would be a simple snatch. We don't have any diplomatic immunity, you know."

"Shut up."

The bleeding man peeled off his coat and grabbed a dish towel from the sink next to the vegetables the woman had been cutting. He pressed the cloth to his side to stanch the flow of blood.

She backed up then, her brain finally communicating the need to flee. But she didn't run. If they heard her, she'd be dead, too. She stepped back into the dining room out of sight. The French doors were right there. Could she make it outside without them seeing her? An icy numbness invaded her every pore, displacing the relaxed euphoria the drugs had created.

Quietly, she crossed the heavy white carpeting, skirting the Queen Anne table and chairs. She shifted her bundle to her other hand and reached for the gold-plated door handle. Blood drummed through her veins so rapidly, she felt deaf. Only the snick of the door latch told her she could still hear. It sounded so loud.

Too loud.

Frightened, she paused. She could hear the hum of their voices in the next room, but not the words. Any moment they would start through the house. She had to run.

In her panic, she forgot that the kitchen also overlooked the patio. She opened the door and skirted the lawn chairs. As her feet touched the grass, she glanced up. Her eyes met those of the injured man as he stood before the window at the sink. His shocked expression probably mirrored her own. She heard him yell. Then she ran.

STEVEN GREGORY opened one bleary eye to peer at the clock. One o'clock. It was only one o'clock. Who would have the nerve to pound on his apartment door at one o'clock in the afternoon?

He'd shoot them, he decided. It would be justifiable homicide. He needed sleep. He absolutely had to have sleep. This was the first time he'd seen the inside of his eyelids in over forty hours. He must sleep. He deserved to sleep. The horrible week had culminated in a horrible night. He'd passed exhaustion a long time ago.

The pounding only increased—both at his front door and in his head. With a vicious oath, Steve swung his long legs off the bed and stumbled over his shoes, then his jeans. For just a second, he debated pulling on the pants. Then he looked down. If the miserable excuse for a human being at his front door had the nerve to wake him, he could take him as he was. Bare-assed naked.

Steve knew a lot of swearwords. Though he rarely used them, he gave vent to several of his favorites as he made his way to the front door. The cops couldn't possibly have more questions. They now knew every detail of the past seventy-two hours, including how often he blinked.

How could they have more questions? And if it wasn't the cops, he would definitely make his caller one sorry individual indeed.

He flung open the door, a blistering comment on his lips. He never uttered it. The sobbing woman had been turning away. Her dark brown hair swung across her face, partially obscuring it as she turned back at the sound of the door opening. The look of hope on her strained features was nearly washed out by the fear. Both emotions were painful to witness in that small pinched face.

Her eyes locked on his.

"Thank God!" she said. "I didn't know what I was going to do. There's no one else home. Here."

Automatically, Steve reached out to take the blanketed bundle she thrust at him.

"I can't wait. My sister should be home any time now. Tell her I'll call and explain."

"Hey! Wait a minute! Where are you going? Hold it!"

A look of utter terror flashed across her features and she fled down the hall to the waiting elevator.

"Get back here!" Steve yelled.

And then the baby began to cry.

Baby?

Steve's gaze dropped to the blanket. He was standing in the hallway of his apartment building, stark naked, holding a crying baby. A very small baby. A very loud, pathetic baby. It was weeping heartrending tears in that high-pitched wail peculiar to infants. Steve wanted to join in. The tiny face screwed tightly in lines of distress, and it vented that distress on his abused eardrums.

"What did I do to deserve this?" He uttered another oath and stared blankly down the now-empty hallway. The baby continued to cry.

This wasn't happening. Maybe he was hallucinating from a lack of sleep. He looked at the tiny bundle in his arms. If so, it was an extremely loud hallucination.

He carried the infant back inside and looked around for a place to set it down. His apartment was furnished in stuff the Salvation Army would reject. There was a ragged wing chair, two smaller chairs and a couple of old crates that served as tables. One lamp had no shade, the other lamp had one, but it was badly ripped and stained. A battered television set perched precariously on a bar stool in the far corner of the room. There was no place to set a baby.

"Great. Just great." The crying infant didn't agree.

The dining area was no better. It held a folding table and six chairs in various stages of disrepair. They were stacked against the scuffed wall.

"Okay, kid, hang on."

Steve strode past the kitchen and into the bedroom where a double bed on a bare frame dominated the square room. A dresser with one drawer missing leaned drunkenly against a wall, and another old crate served as a nightstand. A book, a lamp of a naked lady complete with an intact shade, and a telephone sat on top of the crate. The clock radio sat on the floor.

Steve laid the still-wailing infant on the bed and reached for his pants. Sliding into his rumpled jeans, he grabbed the telephone and dialed.

"O'Hearity Investigations," came the soft, uncertain voice in his ear.

"It's Gregory. Put O'Hearity on the line."

There was a moment's pause while the listener digested that. "Uh, sir, which O'Hearity did you want?"

Steve cursed as he clenched the phone in frustration. Hadn't his call come through on Tim's direct line? Obviously not. "Either one of them. Just put me through."

"I can't," the voice wavered. "They aren't here, sir. Neither one of them. I think Kathy's back there, but she has someone with her. Should I interrupt?"

Steve swallowed a string of oaths. The new receptionist was a girl of eighteen who looked fifteen and had probably been raised by nuns. This was her first work experience.

There was no point in venting his frustration on her. It was her first week on the job and she'd no doubt have hysterics. Besides, it wasn't her fault he was ready to chew through metal. He should have remembered that Tim had left the police station with him in the wee hours of the morning. Tim would be home in bed, just as Steve himself should be. As he had been.

"Never mind."

Steve hung up, debating his options. The baby was crying in earnest now. He unwrapped the blanket to expose a tiny body dressed in some kind of yellow outfit with cutesy little ducks on it. The cutesy little ducks were soaking wet. The baby had done what babies do best. It had made a mess.

He rubbed gritty eyes and thought back to the conversation in the hall. The young woman had been distraught. Had she carried anything with her? Steve scratched his beard. He didn't think she'd even carried a purse, just the baby. No diaper bag, no formula. Nothing.

"Great. Now what am I supposed to do?"

The baby added a decibel to its cries.

"Okay, kid. Hang on."

The woman said her sister was due home at any moment. He knew exactly who she meant. Said sister lived next door to him. He'd recognized the young woman at the door despite her pinched expression. Hard not to. She and his next-door neighbor could almost have been twins—until you saw them up close. There was also a brother that came around occasionally.

The baby's cries tore at his heart. "Okay, little one. Take it easy. I'm thinking as fast as I can."

Thinking, obviously, wasn't going to get the job done. His fingers set about removing the sopping garments. The baby was a girl. A perfectly formed little girl with wispy traces of light-colored hair and the bluest eyes he had ever seen. He washed her off and wrapped her in a soft terry-cloth towel and rocked her gently in his muscled arms. But being dry wasn't enough. The baby continued to cry.

"Okay, kid. Hold on." Probably his neighbor had all the baby's needs inside her locked apartment. "I knew the first time I laid eyes on your aunt she was going to be trouble."

She dressed in prim business suits, and looked every inch the up-and-coming woman executive. She was a slim, pretty woman with a mop of sassy brown hair, but she was not the neighborly type. The first time he saw her, she got her key stuck in the lock of her front door. She snapped at him when he'd offered to help. Of course, she was probably annoyed that he'd been close enough to smell the light scent of her shampoo.

"Well, I was never partial to women with brown hair, in the first place," he told the baby. And this particular mop of brown hair covered an easily dislikable slip of femininity, he'd decided. She grated on his nerves. "She may be cute to look at, but she's rude, condescending and a yuppie." So what did her sister think she was doing, dumping a baby on him?

The baby's pitiful cries demanded attention. The poor little thing was so distressed that Steve found himself shrugging into a sweatshirt and hunting through his tools for his lockpicks. He'd tear a strip off that yuppie when she got home. Meantime, he'd have to break into her apartment to see if he could find his incredible charge a change of clothing.

He wasn't sure whether or not the baby was old enough to roll over, but he wasn't taking any chances.

He set the squalling infant on the floor, out of harm's way, and stomped over to the apartment next door. He had to give his neighbor credit on one count, the woman had good locks. It took several minutes to get inside.

He ran a quick, appraising eye over the room. The lady also had good taste. The apartment was filled with a gentle wash of pastel color, and a light feminine scent that reminded him of her. The furniture invited a person to sit and stay a while and there were wood-framed pictures and small accents dotting the area, but no baby paraphernalia.

"Figures. You aren't going to do anything the easy way, are you?"

The dining area housed a freestanding stereo system, a small round table and four chairs. Nothing remotely like a diaper bag.

The ivory-colored refrigerator was neat and clean, like everything else in the place, and filled with a variety of wholesome foods. His lips curled. There wasn't a single baby bottle and the milk was skim.

Desperate, he opened drawers, doors and cupboards. All of them were neat and tidy and well stocked, but there was still nothing a baby could use.

The bathroom was done in peach and green and the scent he had noticed earlier clung to the air in here. The only thing out of place was the wispy black lace teddy and two black nylons hanging from the shower rod. He fingered the material and found both items were completely dry and silky to the touch. The teddy took his mind in another, more interesting, direction, but the memory of the frantic baby had him turning away.

Her bedroom was like the rest of the apartment except that she hadn't taken the time to make the double bed. Flowered sheets lured him closer. Her scent lingered in the folds to perfume the air of this room, too.

But there was no sign that a baby had ever been here.

Stuffing panic to the back of his mind, Steve lifted a picture from the dresser and studied it. Yep. This was the same young female who had shown up at his door a few moments ago. Next to her stood the woman whose apartment this was, and behind them was a laughing male that could only be their brother. Terrific. That told him absolutely nothing he didn't already know.

Thoughts of the baby had him hastily putting down the picture and dashing back home. Maybe his neighbor was bringing the baby's things back to her apartment with her when she came home. But the child needed attention now.

Steve settled the baby in his arms. Her cries quieted to hiccupy whimpers.

"Sorry, kid. I can't do anything for you in the milk department. Skim milk lowers cholesterol, but somehow I don't think you have to worry about that at this stage of your life."

He continued to rock her with one arm, while with the other he picked up his phone and pushed some familiar numbers.

A woman's voice answered on the first ring. "Petey?"

"Steve? What on earth are you doing up? Tim said you would sleep for hours, if not days, after last night."

Steve sighed. "Don't I wish. Petey, I have a serious problem here. I need your help."

"My help? What's wrong? Should I wake Tim?"

Steve stroked the small cheek of the now-quiet child. He tucked the phone under his chin and adjusted the baby more comfortably against his chest. "No. He can't help. Not yet. I've got a baby and I don't know what to do with her."

Dead silence met this declaration.

Steve sighed audibly and closed his eyes. Petey was Tim's wife. Tim was his boss. Now they would both think he was a moron.

"What I mean is, my next-door neighbor's sister dumped a baby in my arms. It's soaking wet. I don't have anything to dress it in. And it's probably hungry."

He looked down at the child and continued plaintively, "All babies are hungry. They have this empty hole through the middle of their bodies. You put stuff in one end and it comes out the other. In between, they cry and sleep. But then, you know all that. Can you bring something? Lots of somethings. Whatever it takes. I'm sorry, but I really need help until my neighbor shows up."

"Steve," Petey said cautiously, "are you okay?"

"Hell, no!" The baby jumped at his loud tone and began to cry again. He muttered yet another expletive and started rocking the child once more.

"Please, Petey. She's really tiny. I'm betting she's only a few weeks old. I need help."

"I'll be right there," Petey assured him. Steve blessed her for not wasting time asking more questions. "Let me grab a few things we'll need, call the baby-sitter and leave a note for Tim. Hang in there, guy."

"Thanks. I left the front door unlocked. Just come on in when you get here."

SHE FUMBLED in the bag, searching for one of the soothing pills. She knew it was too soon to pop another one, but she didn't care. She needed it. Maybe it would calm her down—help her to decide what to do. Absently, she looked out the window of the apartment.

Her heart sped up so fast it threatened to tear through her chest at any moment. A dark blue sedan pulled up and two men stepped from its interior. Both were wearing suits, and one had thinning red hair. He moved stiffly, painfully.

The killers! How had they found her?

Fool! What did it matter? She had to get out of here.

Frantically, she scrambled into the bedroom. Her hair whipped around her face as she scanned the room. There was no time to pack now. She grabbed the half-filled bag and zipped it shut. Her purse. Where was her purse?

And then she remembered. She had set it on the floor by the chair in the living room. That's how they knew where she lived. They must have found it. They had all her ID, her credit cards, her money, her checkbook, everything. What was she going to do? Who could she turn to?

She stifled a sob of terror. She had to get out of here now. Would they take the steps or the elevator? Would they have someone watching the back entrance?

She threw open the apartment door and ran for the elevator. Ominously, the elevator was already ascending. They were coming. She ran for the stairs. She ran for her life.

"THE MARINES ARE HERE," Petey sang out.

Steve blinked open both eyes instantly at the sound

Steve blinked open both eyes instantly at the sound of Petey's voice, but it was a minute before he actually registered what he'd heard.

"Thank God!"

The baby opened her blue eyes, looked around and began to wail. She had kicked off the makeshift blanket, and when he scooped up the child, he found she was soaked again. So was he. She had wet the bed.

"How can something this small hold so much liquid? It defies the laws of physics or something."

Resigned, he went out to meet his boss's wife.

Petey's own pregnancy was now in its seventh month. Since it would be her second child, she was more than prepared for this emergency and probably any others that involved an infant. One of those bulky infant car seats sat on the living room floor and Steve watched her pull tiny diapers and outfits from the baby bag at her feet. She paused to hand him a bottle filled with milky liquid.

"Warm that for me, will you? About forty seconds in the microwave. And take the nipple off first."

Steve took the bottle and wrinkled his nose. "You aren't really going to give the baby something that smells this bad, are you?"

Petey laughed. "Don't worry, she'll love it."

He shook his head, stepped over his other pair of sneakers and fumbled his way to the kitchen. His brain felt like mush. Catnaps simply made his need for sleep more acute. Only one thing stood out clearly. He wanted to go next door and give his yuppie neighbor the tongue-lashing of her life for putting him in this situation. The rational part of his brain argued that it wasn't her fault. The baby belonged to her sister, after all. Still...

He carried the warmed milk back to the now-screaming infant, and gratefully handed it to the competent woman sitting on the edge of his wing chair.

"I'll be right back," he told her gruffly.

"Where are you going?"

"Next door," he answered grimly. "To the sister's."

At her startled look, he gave Petey a dark smile. "Don't worry. I'm not going to take my gun. Yet."

There was no answer to his repeated pounding on the door next to his. He didn't have to strain his brain for his neighbor's name. He had memorized it the same way he'd memorized her long shapely legs the day she got her key jammed in the mailbox downstairs and glared at him as though it was his fault. Irritating woman.

Obviously, Ms. Jerrilynn Rothmore still hadn't seen fit to come home tonight. Without a qualm, he let himself into her apartment again and went searching for her personal telephone directory. It was in her bedroom in the nightstand on the left-hand side of the bed. He sat on her flowered sheets and tried not to let her elusive scent disturb him.

"The woman's a damn menace." Not only did she wear sexy lingerie and distracting perfume, but she also didn't put down last names in her telephone directory. Her sister could be any of the female names listed. It was hopeless.

Steve had no intention of dialing every female in her book, even if he *was* tempted. Instead, he rummaged until he found a sheet of paper and a pencil. He scrawled Ms. Jerrilynn Rothmore a hasty note and taped it to her front door where she couldn't miss it when she finally did come home.

Petey was calmly feeding the child. She looked up with a gentle smile as he entered. "She's an adorable baby. Any luck?"

"Ms. Rothmore still isn't home. Can you believe it? I'm really sorry to drag you out. I'm thinking of calling the police."

Petey gaped at him. "Whatever for?"

"The sister abandoned this child. Just dumped her in the arms of a total stranger and ran down the hall. She didn't leave me any food or clothing or instructions. All she said was her sister should be home soon. Now, what kind of a mother does that make her?"

"That does sound odd, but maybe we should wait a bit. There could be an extenuating circumstance." Petey frowned. "Maybe your neighbor was delayed or was involved in an accident or something."

"Hah." He snorted. "I should be so lucky. The woman next door is a royal pain. Besides, she doesn't know any more about babies than I do. She doesn't have a single thing inside that apartment for taking care of this child. That makes this an abandoned baby, in my eyes."

Petey raised an eyebrow, and Steve tugged sheepishly at his beard. He smelled of sweat and baby urine, and if he didn't get some sleep soon, he was going to collapse right here on the floor. He swayed slightly. His brain had solidified. He couldn't think straight anymore.

"Why don't you take a quick shower?" she suggested. "After you change your sheets, you can lie down and get some rest. I'll sit here with the baby and listen for your neighbor. If she doesn't come home in a few hours, I'll wake you and you can decide what you want to do."

Steve knew he should argue, but he was just plain too tired. "Thanks, Petey," he said around a yawn. "I can't tell you how much I appreciate this."

His tired brain drifted to his impertinent next-door neighbor and came to rest on the black lace teddy hanging in her bathroom. Was that the sort of thing she wore under all those prim, sexless business suits?

The telephone woke him three hours later.

"What the hell have you done with my wife?"

Steve held the receiver away from his ear and blinked at it. It took him a minute to place the voice and put the question into context. Just then, Petey knocked and stuck her head around his bedroom door as he replied. "I'm holding her for ransom. As soon as I decide on my needs, I'll tell you the terms."

"You're fired," Tim told him, seemingly unperturbed. "What's this about a baby? I'm exhausted, so I'm probably not reading this note right, but you should be comatose after that melee last night and the hours of surveillance before it."

"I am. And I *was* sleeping until you woke me with this stupid phone call. Your wife is right here."

"Now you're a dead man," Tim warned him.

"And that is no joke, boss," he responded. He held out the phone to Petey and said loudly, "I think your husband suspects something."

She took the receiver and handed him the baby in exchange, giving him a playful swat. "How come you're awake?" she asked her husband.

"How come you're in Steve's bedroom?"

Tim's voice carried clearly to where Steve sat.

"I had to take care of the baby," she told him reasonably.

"So your note says. Whose baby?"

"I don't think we know for sure yet."

She explained the little she knew and added that the neighbor had not yet come home.

"Let me talk to him."

Phone and baby traded hands once again and Steve tugged at his beard. "I think you'd better call the cops," Tim told him.

"I think so, too." He looked at the sleeping child. She was such a sweet, innocent little baby. It didn't feel right to turn the helpless infant over to some government agency. "I'll give my neighbor until seven-thirty, then I'll call."

"Why seven-thirty?" Tim wanted to know.

He shrugged, but his eyes had strayed to the baby in Petey's arms.

"I said, why seven-thirty?" Tim repeated. "Why don't you call the authorities now?"

"Because my neighbor usually comes home around seven or seven-thirty."

"And I suppose she has red hair," Tim said in resignation.

Steve snorted. "No way. She isn't my type at all. Medium brown hair—" that drifted carelessly, making a man want to smooth it back "—medium height—" with eyes that hinted at a hidden knowledge a man just had to discover "—medium business suits—" that covered enticing bits of lace and silk "—medium everything. She's a perfect yuppie with her nose stuck so high in the air she has a permanent nosebleed."

Tim chortled. "Wouldn't give you the time of day, huh?"

Steve found himself grinning in response. "Nope. You'd think I carried typhoid. Snotty little thing. Just because I borrowed her newspaper one morning."

"Uh-huh. Well, put my wife back on. The baby-sitter has to leave and Laura wants her dinner."

A few minutes later, Steve found himself abandoned in the overstuffed wing chair with the tiny infant curled contentedly in his arms. A pile of baby paraphernalia littered the card table, and a list of instructions—including the name and phone number of a pediatrician "just in case"—sat on top of everything.

By eight-fifteen, Steve had picked up and replaced the telephone several times. He knew he should call the authorities, but the baby was such a sweetheart, he couldn't bring himself to do it.

"Like Petey said," he told the baby, "maybe there's a good explanation for this." The baby yawned. "Yeah, my thoughts exactly."

He kept taking catnaps with the child in his arms, but by nine-fifteen, he decided it was time to take serious action. He carried the baby with him as he went next door and picked the lock. His note was no longer on the door.

The cool living room had changed. For one thing, there was a light on. For another, a large beige suitcase squatted on the floor not far from the door. Down the hall, he could hear the sound of the shower running. Jerrilynn Rothmore had returned at last. She must have come home when he dozed off the last time, Steve decided. And she must have the baby stuff in that suitcase. Well, fine. He needed sleep, by heaven, and she could pay him for baby-sitting. What kind of an aunt was she? Why hadn't she come over as soon as she got his note?

As the shower continued to run, Steve's anger mounted. Just who did this woman think she was? She didn't deserve to take care of this baby. It would serve her right if he just left and reported the two of them to the police. Come to think of it, where was the baby's father?

The shower stopped and Steve started down the hall toward the bathroom. He wasn't going to stand around any longer like some flunky. He needed sleep. At least twenty-four hours' worth. Ms. Jerrilynn Rothmore could have her niece back right now. He was outta here.

The odor of shampoo he had noticed earlier was much stronger now, wafting down the hall to tantalize him. She had left the bathroom door open, and Steve's senses were completely assaulted as soon as he reached the room. All of his senses came under fire, but his eyes took a direct hit.

She stood in the center of the fluffy green carpet, wiping her body with a large peach-colored towel. She had one of the most perfect bodies he had ever seen—and he was seeing all of it. Her skin was a gorgeous pink shade, beaded with water droplets. She was formed just the way a woman should be formed. She was incredible.

His skin prickled under the steamy heat pouring from the small room and his body added its own heat at the sight in front of him. His mouth could almost taste the scent that his nose was telling him came from the open bottle of lotion sitting on the vanity. This was a man's dream come true.

It was her healthy, extremely loud scream that brought him back to reality and did the damage. It woke the baby in his arms.

"Now look what you've done," he snapped as she scrambled to cover herself. "You woke her up again.

Damn it, woman. You've got five minutes to throw on some clothes and then I'm going to call the police."

"*What?*"

Her shocked outrage trailed after him as he went back into the living room and tried to force out of his mind the memory of that lush figure. Who would have thought his yuppie neighbor was built along those lines? He never would have guessed she looked so good underneath those double-breasted suits she wore all the time. He probably should have suspected it, though, after seeing the teddy and the black hose earlier.

"Get out before I call the police!"

"Now, there's an idea."

"How did you get in here? What do you want? Get out!"

She stood in the hall with the fluffy peach towel wrapped securely around her body. It covered her strategically, while another towel encompassed her hair. Her gray eyes were enormous against her flushed skin and her lips were trembling with emotion.

"You want me out?" he asked. "Fine."

He set the squalling infant on the white-marshmallow couch, braced her with a pillow so she couldn't roll off and headed for the door. "I'm gone. She's your problem now. Be aware that I am the one who'll be calling the police to report your sister for reckless abandonment, and I will be sending you the bill for my services. My boss's wife can bill you for her time and the clothing and formula and whatnot. I don't know what she'll charge, but I've had the baby since one o'clock this afternoon, and I get fifty dollars an hour plus expenses."

"*What?*" she screamed. "What are you doing? Where are you going? You can't leave that baby *here!*"

"Can, and am." Steve opened the front door and added, "Don't worry, the police will no doubt take her away from you as soon as they arrive." He slammed the door as he left.

Lynn looked from the squalling infant to the front door and back again. "Has the world gone completely mad today? What's going on?"

The baby calmed down immediately when she picked up the infant. "You're a beautiful baby, but who do you belong to?"

What on earth had he meant about her sister and calling the police? What had Marcy done now?

Lynn carried the baby into the bedroom and laid her on the bed while she quickly dug through her closet for something to wear. What a hateful man. Fifty dollars an hour plus expenses, indeed. If the bearded man even had a job—which she seriously doubted—he worked strange hours and he probably made minimum wage. She'd seen the way he dressed and that clunker he drove around in.

He dressed like a bum, usually in faded blue jeans and rumpled sweatshirts or decrepit sweat suits. True, the jeans did mold a rather shapely rear end and the sweatshirts did nothing to disguise the breadth of those shoulders. But she hated that horrid beard he wore and he needed a haircut. He was a long way from the gentle, sophisticated men she knew and dated. She'd bet he didn't even own a tie.

And he had stood in her bathroom ogling her naked body. She nearly trembled at the memory. It was not because of desire, she assured herself. It was anger, pure and simple.

Besides, it didn't matter. At least he hadn't acted as if it mattered, afterward. Lynn snorted. It did not matter. She didn't care a fig what he thought. But if he believed he was going to dump this poor little baby in her lap, he'd better try thinking again.

When she'd arrived home, she had read the note he had taped to her front door, but it hadn't made any sense. She was tired and had no intention of knocking on his door and discussing something that appeared to be an obvious mistake.

"Hang it all. I'm supposed to be on an airplane to California right this minute." Only they'd overbooked the plane and the ticket agent claimed they had lost her reservation. It was the final straw in a long day. She had just spent the last twenty-some hours in meetings and airports, only to be told she couldn't board the plane. That meant she couldn't make the meeting that she didn't want to attend in the first place.

Lynn struggled into a pair of slacks and looked down at the smiling infant. No, she amended, *this* was the final straw. "A baby. What am I supposed to do with a baby, for heaven's sake? I don't know anything about babies."

The impossible man had mentioned Marcy. Well, what on earth could Marcy possibly have to do with a baby? Lynn ran a comb through her wet hair and picked up the phone next to her bed. When her sister's answering machine finished playing its greeting, she fired off her message.

"You'd better call me right now, Marcy. I'm not kidding. I'm at home and I'm furious. My neighbor is talking about calling the police. I want to know about this baby and I want to know right now. Call me."

She hung up and looked down at the infant. "If that dumb jerk from next door thinks he's going to intimidate me, he has another think coming."

All day, Lynn had been dealing with airline personnel and corporate bosses. She had had plenty of practice handling intimidating people. She slipped into tennis shoes and lifted the tiny bundle into her arms. It really was a beautiful baby.

"Sorry, sweetie. It's nothing personal."

Her neighbor claimed he had taken the baby from Marcy, so it was up to her neighbor to deal with the consequences. She snatched up her key, made sure her door was shut and locked securely, and pounded on the door next to hers.

"This is not my baby," she announced when he finally opened his door. "Here."

He dropped his hands to his sides and backed up. "Oh, no, you don't. That's what your sister pulled. I may be falling-down tired, but I'm not stupid enough to fall for that trick twice."

Lynn stepped inside the almost-barren apartment. The room was one mini step away from absolute squalor. Her gaze took in the surroundings and quickly riveted back on the bearded face in front of her.

"If Marcy gave you this baby, then that's between the two of you. Don't get me involved."

He looked at her as if she had lost her mind. "What the hell kind of people are you? You want me to turn over your sister's baby to the authorities? Lady, you're really something. I knew you were a cold piece of work, but this is incredible."

"My sister's baby?" she shrieked. "My sister doesn't have a baby!"

The baby began to cry.

"See what you did," Steve scolded.

"What I did? What *I* did?" For a moment, Lynn thought she would hit him with something. Obviously he thought so, too, because he reached out and took the wailing child. Immediately, the baby quieted.

Steve wasn't wearing a shirt any longer, and his broad chest was firmly muscled and covered in a mat of fine dark hair. Lynn had never cared for hairy chests, but there was something almost compelling about this one. She was amazed at how comfortable this big burly man looked, holding such a tiny bundle. She gave herself a mental kick and looked up into dark brown eyes.

"Do you think," she asked carefully, "we could start over again? I don't have a clue as to what is going on here. I'm supposed to be halfway to San Francisco right now. My sister either isn't home or isn't answering her telephone, but I assure you, this baby isn't hers. She isn't even married."

"I don't think that's mandatory anymore."

"I beg your pardon?"

"Marriage. She doesn't have to be married to have a baby."

Lynn clenched her jaw and tried counting to ten. He was exasperating. Totally maddening. "Very true. However, when I saw Marcy the week before last, she didn't have a baby or any plans to acquire one."

Quiet now, its tiny fingers curled trustingly around one of Steve's enormous ones, the baby regarded him with an unblinking stare. Even at her young age, she appeared mesmerized by the potency of this man.

"Then where did this baby come from?" he asked in a soft voice.

Lynn looked from the man to the child and back again. "I haven't got a clue."

Chapter Two

"What are we going to do now? It's all gone wrong and we're going to get caught!"

The red-haired man studied his companion, wishing his side didn't hurt so badly. He resented having to deal with this right now when he needed time to think, but the fellow did have a point. He'd planned it all so carefully, how had it all gone so wrong?

"We don't have a choice."

"But it isn't going to work," the other man protested. "We've got to find that bloody girl and the baby."

That much was a fact. They must find the baby whether they found the girl or not, but it would be best if they found both of them. He pressed his hand to his side, hoping to ease the pain. It didn't help.

"Don't lose your nerve," he told the other man. "We'll find her. She didn't go to the authorities." He paused to consider this. "I wonder why," he mused aloud.

"What difference does it make? How are we going to find her? We've phoned nearly everyone on this bleeding list." He waved the small red notebook with its unhelpful list of telephone numbers in the air. Then he smacked it down on the table next to the girl's oversized purse. "It's bloody hopeless."

"No, she went to ground with the baby somewhere. We have her credit cards and her money, so how far can she go? We only have to think logically. Perhaps it would be best if you go back to her place and keep watch. I have a feeling she'll return there eventually. Don't worry. We'll get the baby and go home soon enough."

WITH MUCH RELUCTANCE, Lynn had agreed to keep the baby overnight rather than call the police. No doubt the starkness of his apartment appalled her delicate sensibilities, he thought. Steve didn't care what her reason was, he just wanted some uninterrupted sleep. He finally got it—even if his last conscious thoughts were of his next-door neighbor in her steamy bathroom with droplets of water clinging to her delectable skin.

They'd agreed to meet around nine the next morning. By then, Jerrilynn declared, her sister would have called to explain. Steve hoped she was right.

He felt like a new man after eight hours of sleep, a relaxing shower and a change of clothes. He dressed in his best pair of black jeans, a new blue shirt and a clean black sweatshirt. Not that he dressed to impress his neighbor, he assured himself, but he felt a need to look neat. He and Tim had been on this last case for so long it was hard to remember what it felt like to dress in decent clothing.

He combed his hair and his beard and studied the results. Not bad. He could use a haircut, though, and he was getting pretty tired of the beard. Steve shrugged. This was as good as he was going to get for today.

When Jerrilynn finally opened the door to his knock, he decided he looked a lot better than she was likely to notice.

Jerrilynn was wearing a long, print robe of muted colors that molded itself to her shapely body. It was stained where the baby had regurgitated on it more than once. Her hair hung in limp tangles around her delicate shoulders, and her eyes were sunken holes in her pale creamy skin. Lines of strain had formed on her face. Lines that hadn't been there the night before. She looked rumpled and disgruntled and completely exhausted. He had to suppress a surprising urge to reach out and comfort her.

"You," she snapped by way of greeting. "How could you do this to me?"

"What?"

"That child has been up most of the night. All she does is cry. I don't know what she wants. Do you know what kind of a week I've had? Do you know how badly I need sleep?"

He managed to stifle a smile.

"I don't know anything about babies. If I had a gun, I'd shoot you. And when I get my hands on my sister, I'm going to strangle her." Her fingers fluttered at her sides as her anger mounted. He watched with interest as her breasts rose and fell beneath the thin robe.

"Maybe I'll push her out the window, or I could tie her to some railroad tracks. Whatever would be most painful, I don't care."

Steve's amusement grew. This was a completely new side to his classy, refined neighbor. Steve would take bets that very few people caught a glimpse of this aspect of Jerrilynn Rothmore. He decided he liked it. She was more human and approachable this way. There was a hidden fire beneath the veneer. Jerrilynn would be a sexy lady if she ever turned loose of all that repressed passion.

"You need coffee," Steve told her, stepping inside the quiet apartment. "Where's the baby?"

Lynn muttered something he didn't catch and motioned toward her bedroom. He sauntered in that direction and found the infant sleeping peacefully in the center of the brightly flowered sheets.

"Now she sleeps," Lynn grumbled. "All night long she fussed and fumed and now she sleeps."

Steve grinned. "She's probably worn-out," he told her unrepentantly. "Why don't you go get a shower and I'll make you some coffee. I take it you haven't heard from your sister yet?"

Her expressive face stilled instantly. "No. Frankly, last night I wasn't worried. My sister is... well..."

"An airhead?"

Lynn bristled, then sighed. "I swear to God, she never thinks anything through. I called all her friends I could think of and no one has seen her. But then, she has a lot of friends and I only know a few of them."

Steve didn't respond. He stood in her hallway and studied her face. Her fingers played nervously with the belt on her robe, and he wondered what she was wearing under that sexy bit of material. It had a mighty tempting zipper all the way down the front.

Lynn cleared her throat nervously. "When Marcy didn't answer her phone this morning, I started growing concerned. Mom and Dad are in Australia so there's no point calling them, and I think this was the week my brother left for England on business."

She stared into space for a moment, then her mouth firmed decisively. "I think we should drive over there."

Amused, he leaned back against the wall and asked, "To England?"

"No," she said, exasperated. "To my sister's."

Steve swallowed a chuckle. He reached out to tap Lynn gently under the chin, an action that surprised both of them. There was a tingling of sudden awareness. He could see it was mutual. A hint of color sat high on her cheeks, flushing the skin that had been pale only moments ago.

"Better get your shower, Jerrilynn. You'll be more coherent after coffee and a shower."

That broke the ridiculous spell immediately. Her features tightened and she stepped forward so she was only inches from him. She pointed a long, manicured fingernail in the direction of his broad chest.

"Nobody calls me Jerrilynn. The name is Lynn."

He studied her narrowed eyes and found he was grinning again. She was a fierce little thing when riled. "Why not? I kinda like Jerrilynn. It's different."

"It's ridiculous." She tossed her head back regally and continued to glower at him. When he didn't move, her anxiety took on another meaning entirely. He could see the knowledge grow on her face. They were, after all, standing very close together in a narrow hallway. It wouldn't take much for him to lean down and place a definitive kiss on those very uncertain lips. It was tempting. Almost too tempting.

When she drew in a deep lungful of air, his breath caught in his chest as her breasts swelled invitingly. Then her eyes narrowed and she pushed against him with one hand before storming silently past him and into the bathroom. The door slammed behind her.

Steve expelled his breath in a chuckle. Fortunately, she hadn't disturbed the baby. A smile stayed on his lips as he went in search of her coffeepot. For a woman with brown hair instead of red, Lynn certainly had a temper.

"YOU WERE RIGHT," she told him in grudging amazement a half hour later. She stood in the kitchen doorway, fastening a crystal earring to one earlobe.

Steve set down his coffee cup, taking in the transformation. She was dressed in crisp linen slacks that accented the length of those gorgeous legs. The tailored white blouse with the navy cardigan couldn't conceal the curves underneath. Her sassy brown hair curled jauntily around her face, just begging to be touched.

"I do feel better. But," she warned him, "I am still tired and I am not going to keep this baby another night."

He bit into the cinnamon toast he had made and nodded as she took a seat across from him and lifted a coffee cup to her lips.

"I agree. If we can't find your sister, we need to call the authorities. For all we know, she kidnapped the baby."

"Kidnapped!" The coffee cup clunked to the table, sloshing liquid across the wooden surface in every direction and soaking into the brightly colored cloth place mats. Lynn seemed oblivious. "What do you mean, kidnapped? My sister is a flake, not a criminal. Marcy wouldn't kidnap anyone."

Steve met her hostility with a bland look before he stood and reached for a paper towel to mop up some of the spill. She snatched the towel from his hands and continued to glare accusingly.

"Maybe," he agreed noncommittally. "I don't know your sister or what she's capable of, but I do know that she was one upset lady yesterday."

Lynn sputtered for a moment, but then sat quietly as his words sank in. "Did she say anything?"

"Just what I told you."

"She must be doing a favor for a friend."

He raised an eyebrow. "By leaving a baby with a total stranger?"

The ringing of the telephone was so loud and unexpected, both of them jumped. Lynn jerked to her feet with a speed that nearly overturned her chair.

"It's probably Marcy now. She can explain everything. And it had better be a real good explanation for this. Hello?"

"Marcellina Rothmore?"

"She isn't here. Who's calling, please?"

"A friend. Do you happen to know where I can reach her?"

Lynn coiled the telephone cord tensely between her fingers. "No. I'm trying to find her, myself. Who is this?"

"Thank you."

"Wait!" But she was talking to an empty line. Tendrils of fear licked along her nerve endings. There had been nothing in the words spoken by the quiet voice to make her feel so frightened, but she couldn't deny the emotion.

"Who was it?" Steve asked. "What's wrong?"

She turned to stare at him for a moment. "It was a man," she told him quietly. "He wanted Marcy."

"Did he give you his name?"

Absently, she shook her head, and he reached up to brush aside a lock of hair that had lodged against her cheek. His hand dropped away and she found she wanted to reach for it and hold on. It was a silly reaction. "No, and I didn't recognize the voice."

Steve frowned. "Then why are you so upset?"

Lynn looked at him then. Really looked at him. There was a half-tamed quality to this man. It was like facing a well-fed panther in your living room. His dark eyes watched her, filled with concern. She found herself trying to explain. "It was his voice. I don't know. There was something about his voice that made me think..."

"What?"

"I don't know. It was a quiet voice. He didn't say anything threatening. Only, why did he call here looking for Marcy? Come to think of it, how did he know to call here? Where did he get my number? If it was one of her friends, why didn't he identify himself?"

He laid a comforting hand on her arm. "Tell me exactly what he said."

She was very conscious of that hand. "Something's wrong. I know it."

Steve steered her back to her chair, resisting an urge to leave his hand where it was as she repeated the brief telephone conversation. "He asked for Marcellina. Marcellina, not Marcy." Her bright red fingernails tapped a staccato beat on the Formica tabletop. "A salesperson would do that, not anyone who knows her. I just have a bad feeling about this."

So did he, but Steve didn't want to add to her concern. "It could have been anyone. Maybe it's a new boyfriend. She probably mentioned your name and he looked it up in the phone book."

"I have an unlisted number." Abruptly, she stood to begin clearing the table. "We need to go over to her place. Maybe she's home and just not answering the phone. We'll take my car. You can take the baby."

A smile tugged at the corners of his lips. She was a mercurial woman, but he liked that she was quick to form a plan of action. She was thinking again instead of reacting.

"We could take my truck," he offered.

Lynn stopped rinsing her cup to glare at him. "Is that what it is? I did wonder." She went back to cleaning the kitchen with brisk, efficient movements. "No, thanks. I like to travel in a vehicle that will get me where I'm going. That multihued death trap you drive is lucky to make it out of the parking lot."

His smile widened. He was beginning to genuinely like this woman.

"It's primer," he told her. "I'm going to paint it one of these days. I just bought it recently, and it runs fine. It was a steal. Once I get it painted, it'll look great."

Lynn pursed her lips in disbelief. "If you paid money for it, it wasn't a steal, it was a crime. Maybe you can prosecute."

Steve found his lips were twitching. "It runs great," he defended.

"If you say so. We'll still take my car," she insisted.

"Okay. If driving means that much to you, far be it from me to argue."

"Good." She took the coffee-soaked rag from his hands. "Besides, I know where we're going."

"Oh, yeah?" At his throaty words, her lips parted in surprise. "Where's that, Jerrilynn?"

She ignored the mischief behind his provocative tone.

"To my sister's," she announced firmly. "Get the baby."

Steve winked, noting her high color before sauntering down the hall to collect the baby and the bag of items Petey had brought over. This could prove to be an interesting afternoon. He and Lynn together in the confines of her small car? Yes, indeed, an interesting afternoon.

LYNN OWNED an Acura, of course. A quiet, subdued, silver-gray car that fit the image of an up-and-coming executive. As they struggled to figure out how to set the child carrier into position, he kept getting whiffs of her subtle fragrance that stirred an unbidden reaction in him. When his fingers brushed hers as they fumbled to get the seat belt around the carrier, Lynn pulled back and quickly averted her eyes. She was apparently no more immune to this strange attraction than he was.

The car ran with smooth precision, and she handled it with quiet competence despite her obvious awareness of his presence. Steve shifted so his shoulder nearly touched hers and she stiffened. Conquering an urge to grin, he stretched out an arm, taunting her by tapping his fingers on the headrest, close to the back of her neck.

"Do you mind?" she muttered.

"Not at all."

She pursed her prim lips and he twisted away so she wouldn't see him smile. Oh, yes, she was aware of him, all right.

Traffic was heavy as they headed out of Bethesda. After a while, they pulled up in front of a new apartment complex in Germantown. Lynn couldn't seem to get out of the car fast enough. Carrying the baby seat, he followed her inside the tall brick building, enjoying the seductive sway of her hips. An intriguing woman, for all her haughty airs.

"If you have keys to your sister's place, does she have a set to yours?" he asked, shifting the heavy carrier to his other arm.

"Uh-huh. My whole family has keys to one another's places in case of emergency. Why?"

"I'm just being nosy."

Lynn led the way to a bank of elevators, conscious of the impossible man at her back. He stood too close to her in the elevator, making her aware once again of how good he smelled and what a large man he was.

She was glad when the elevator doors opened. Marcy's apartment was on the fifth floor at the end of the hall. Lynn had the key out, ready to insert it in the lock, when Steve covered her fingers with his. She looked at his forbidding expression and froze.

"Here. Take the baby." He spoke quietly as he reached out and handed her the carrier. His body radiated tension. The panther had changed in the blink of an eye. All of a sudden, he loomed before her, tall and menacing. And tough. Very tough. He looked the part of a sleek, dangerous predator.

"Get behind me," he ordered softly.

His features brooked no argument. She stepped back, questions ready to spring from her lips. They were never uttered. Steve nudged her. "Get over near the stairs," he whispered. He didn't wait to see if she complied.

Right before her eyes, her easygoing bum of a neighbor had turned into a cop. Not, of course, that he was one—surely he would have mentioned the fact before now. Still, it was what came to mind as he flattened himself against the wall.

There was a coiled strength about Steve as he paused there to listen. Lynn had done what he'd told her. Now she gave a quiet gasp as he pushed on the door to Marcy's apartment with the flat of his hand. He hadn't needed the key. The door swung open.

Steve entered fast and low, just as she'd seen actors do in movies and on television. There was a sudden yelp and a crash. Fear for Steve made her want to rush forward, but her responsibility to the baby riveted her to the nearest door. From her position, she couldn't see a thing.

"Steve?"

He didn't respond.

Something crawly nested in her stomach. Her harsh breathing echoed in her ears. Her hands were slick with fear. There were no sounds from inside her sister's apartment. Oh, God, what if something horrible had happened to him?

Carefully, she inched forward along the wall. When she reached the open door, she stopped moving altogether. A gasp burst past her lips.

The contents of the apartment had been thoroughly destroyed. Not a single item remained standing. Anything easily broken, had been. Steve reappeared from the back of the apartment, pausing to rub his shin. It didn't take a genius to guess that he had tripped over the coffee table and probably landed on the broken lamp.

"Come on in," he told her. "It's clean."

She looked at him blankly. "What?"

"There's no one here now," he translated. "I take it this isn't your sister's usual style of decorating?"

Lynn shifted her feet, too rattled to answer him. Her eyes roamed his body. Steve was okay. Relief was immediately replaced by fear for her sister.

"What happened here? Where's Marcy?"

"I don't know. We need to call the police."

Panic overwhelmed her. "No! We can't." She thought about her missing sister and the baby as she regarded the disaster. "Not until I talk to Marcy."

Steve stood an upholstered chair upright and motioned for her to sit down. He turned over another chair and found the seat cushion. Then he sat and watched as she freed the fussing baby and lifted her onto one shoulder to pat her back.

"Lynn, your sister is obviously in trouble. Maybe serious trouble."

Steve waited, but Lynn wouldn't look at him. She shifted the baby to cradle it in her arms. When she raised her head, there was a hint of moisture in those feather gray eyes. A tight knot formed in his gut.

"She wouldn't do anything really wrong." Lynn's expression pleaded for understanding. "Sometimes she acts before she thinks, but Marcy doesn't have a mean bone in her body."

"Maybe not, but someone does." He motioned to the rubble around them.

Lynn stared at him.

"Still think she didn't kidnap this baby?"

Lynn's chin came up, a defiant look in her eyes. "She didn't. She wouldn't."

"But...?" he prodded.

Lynn looked down at the child. Lifting her eyes to his, she said, "It's possible her friend Kevin did and she's covering for him. Only, why would he trash her apartment like this?"

Steve sighed. "Who's Kevin?"

"Kevin Goldlund. He lives here in the building." Lynn wrinkled her nose.

"You don't approve of him? Or where he lives?"

Lynn met his look and her glare was enough of an answer. "He can live anywhere he wants to. I just wish he wasn't dating my sister."

"Why? What do you know about him?"

"Not much, and all of it bothers me. She's been dating him for the past several months. It's changed her."

"How?"

Lynn shrugged. She didn't want to go into all the little ways Marcy had changed. While she sensed Steve was a man she could confide in, it seemed wrong to tell him personal details about her sister.

"I don't trust Kevin. Marcy brought him to a party at my place one night. Later, I discovered several items missing."

"Expensive stuff?"

"A gold necklace and some sapphire earrings I had left out on the bedroom dresser."

Steve stroked his beard. "You think Kevin took them?"

Lynn shrugged, trying to keep her expression blank. "There are other possibilities, but that one did come to mind. I think even Marcy has begun to have second thoughts about their relationship. They've been fighting a lot."

"Okay. What's his apartment number?"

"I don't know. Why?"

"I'm going to pay a call on him. When I get back, we'll call the police."

She looked stricken. She glanced around the room at the mess and bit down on her lower lip. With an anguished expression, her gaze drifted to the tiny infant.

"That sweet little girl belongs to someone," Steve reminded her softly. "How would you feel if it was your daughter who was missing and you didn't know where she was—or even if she was safe?"

Lynn didn't raise her head, but Steve saw the sparkle of a silent tear as it made its way down her cheek. He rose from his chair and laid a gentle hand on her shoulder. He could feel her trembling, fighting for control.

"It'll be okay, Lynn." He saw her nod and began to prowl the apartment. He understood her fear, and he admired her loyalty. But the fact was, after seeing this apartment, they needed to talk to the police and they needed to do it right away.

The phone trilled somewhere beneath the mess at his feet. Its noise shocked him, coming out of nowhere like that. It took him a second to find the instrument half-buried under a chair cushion.

Lynn watched, her face ravaged and tense. Steve hesitated, but her look encouraged him, so he lifted the receiver.

"Hello." There was a sudden gasp, then a moment of silence and then a click as the other person hung up.

"Who was it?" Lynn asked.

Steve shrugged and looked away from her expectant gray eyes. He didn't want to tell her that he strongly suspected it had been her sister.

"I should have had you answer it. Whoever it was probably would have responded to a female voice."

Steve traced the cord and found the phone had an answering machine attached. The police were not going to be happy with him for disturbing evidence this way, but he righted the stand. Then he placed the phone and machine back on it and depressed the play button.

Instantly, a man's voice filled the room with menace. "I want it back, Marcy. I know you took it. Bring it here within the next hour or I'll make you sorry you were ever born, do you read me?"

Lynn met Steve's eyes fearfully. "That was Kevin," came her anguished whisper. "Oh, my God, what has Marcy done?"

The next voice was feminine, light and bubbly and sounding very young to Steve's jaded ears. "Hey, there, Marcy, it's Sue. Just wondered how ya made out with that interview. Gimme a call when you can. Oh, by the way, some guy called here lookin' for you. How'd he get my name? He wouldn't give me his, but he sounded real cool, ya know? You finally dump ole Kev or what? Gimme a call. Bye-ee."

Steve looked at her, but Lynn simply shrugged, unable to identify the caller. The next two messages were the ones she had left for her sister last night and early this morning. There was one final call. Steve tipped his head and Lynn leaned forward as they both strained to hear the words.

"Don't report what you saw. I want her back, or I'll kill you."

"Oh, God." Lynn covered her mouth with a shaking hand.

It was impossible to tell if the voice belonged to a man or woman. Steve replayed the message, trying to hear more clearly. More than likely, he or she had something covering the mouthpiece. The caller must have used a pay phone. There were a lot of traffic sounds in the background, but nothing Steve could use to pin down the location.

"Any idea who that was?" he asked.

Lynn shook her head, her eyes enormous against her pale skin. Steve probed some debris absently with his foot. He took out a clean handkerchief and wiped off the phone and the surfaces he had touched.

"You said you called all her friends you could think of. Do you know who Sue is?"

"No. Marcy's always going to parties and meeting people."

He grimaced. "A social butterfly like her sister, huh? Okay. Where does she keep her address book?"

Lynn wanted to take umbrage at his comment, but there was a kernel of truth to the description. Lynn did have a lot of friends and did quite a lot of entertaining, even if much of it was business-oriented. She was surprised that he had noticed. And also just a tiny bit pleased by that fact.

She and Marcy were nothing at all alike, however. Marcy lived a carefree existence. Their parents supplemented the cost of this apartment so Marcy could experience independent living. Lynn was willing to acknowledge that, as the baby of the family, Marcy had been spoiled by everyone.

"What do you want with her address book?" she asked, pausing for a moment before continuing. "I think she keeps it in her purse."

"We need to see who she knows that you don't. The police will want a list of all her friends. An address book would be a big help. It appears we aren't the only ones searching for her. This is probably pointless, but why don't you have a look around and see if anything obvious is missing."

"What are you going to do?"

"Go downstairs and find out Kevin's apartment number. I want to have a chat with him."

She studied him doubtfully. "I'll go with you."

"Oh no, you won't. You'll stay right here."

Her chin came up, eyes blazing. "No way. She's my sister."

"No one would doubt it for a moment. However, that isn't the point. I don't need the distraction of the baby when I see Kevin. I can intimidate him a lot better if I'm not playing Mr. Rogers." He nodded at the infant. "Are you going to let me handle this or do you plan to give me another headache?"

Lynn glared at him, but there was also concern in her expression. "What do you mean by intimidate him? You heard his message. Kevin sounds crazy. You aren't going to do anything stupid, are you?"

"Probably. You seem to have that effect on me." He held up his hand in a placating gesture when she would have objected. She was scared and she was concerned. He liked the fact that some of the concern seemed to be for him. "Look, I'm just going to talk to him, see if he knows where Marcy is. Then we'll call the police. Agreed?"

Their eyes met and held.

"Okay, agreed. But you'll be careful?"

"I didn't know you cared," he teased. Her eyes widened as he trailed a knuckle down her soft cheek. Without waiting for a response, he stepped quickly out into the hall.

If only he'd been more alert yesterday when Marcy had handed him the baby. Hindsight is lousy, but he couldn't forget the expression on Marcy's face when she ran from him. At the time, he thought it was because she had suddenly realized he was nude. Now, he wasn't so sure. In retrospect, he didn't think her eyes had ever drifted lower than the baby in his arms. Now, *there* was a pin to burst his ego.

He knew Lynn didn't want to call the police. She wanted to protect her sister. Well, he didn't want to call the cops, either, but they needed to find out what was going on.

Steve sincerely hoped Kevin was home.

A quick check of the mailboxes revealed Marcy's boyfriend lived on the second floor on the other side of the building. There was no response to Steve's knock, so he spent a couple of minutes working on the lock before he could let himself inside the apartment.

Shock held him still. He gazed around the empty room. Kevin not only wasn't home, Kevin was gone permanently, leaving only dirt and dust behind.

Steve prowled the stripped apartment, opening doors and cupboards. It wasn't until he looked in the kitchen that he found any signs of the person who had lived here. Kevin had forgotten to empty the refrigerator. There was beer, pop, leftover pizza, butter, milk and some miscellaneous items. The pint of milk was dated two days ago and only half of it was gone. In the freezer he found two full ice trays, a carton of fudge-ripple ice cream and some frozen dinners.

Scrupulously, Steve wiped his prints off the refrigerator and glared around the room. There wasn't anything more to be learned here, so he headed back to the elevator. Lynn was not going to be pleased. Whatever her sister had gotten herself involved in, it was now way past time to call the police.

He was thinking of Lynn's reaction to the news when he stepped off the elevator into the hallway. As he started toward Marcy's apartment, however, his pulse sped up and he broke into a run. Her apartment door gaped wide open.

"Lynn?"

There was no answer to his shout. A quick search proved what he'd already known would be true. There was no one in the apartment. Steve cursed, even as he sprinted for the elevator. She'd run. He hadn't expected this. He knew Lynn didn't want to call the police, but he'd been sure she'd understood. If nothing else, the baby's need for its parents should have convinced her. He hadn't thought Lynn would protect her sister at the expense of the child.

All the way downstairs in the elevator he cursed himself for a fool. He should never have gotten involved. He should have called the cops last night when Marcy first dumped the baby in his arms. He knew better. Hell, if the baby was kidnapped, he could lose his license. The police department frowned heavily on private investigators who didn't play by the rules—particularly if they got caught.

Even as he raced out into the sunshine, he told himself it was pointless. Lynn would be long gone by now. She'd probably left as soon as he'd gone downstairs.

The sight of her silver Acura gleaming in the sunshine brought him up short. It sat in the parking lot right where they had left it, empty.

Baffled, he looked around the lot. Where the heck had she gone? Nerves danced along his spine and tension lent wings to his feet. No, damn it. Marcy's apartment had been empty. He'd checked it.

But he hadn't checked the stairwell.

This time, he took the stairs, his body flooded with adrenaline.

Lynn stood in the apartment doorway looking annoyed. She held the baby carrier in one hand and a slip of paper in another. Excitement fairly exploded from her as she saw him.

"I knew she wouldn't kidnap anyone. Look. See what I found?" she began without preamble, waving the slip of paper. "I knew there had to be an explanation. Where were you?"

Steve stood perfectly still, trying to bring his breathing under control. "Where was I? Where were you? I thought you ran."

"What do you mean, you thought I ran? Ran where? Why?"

Steve knew he was in trouble no matter how he answered that one. He stepped forward and reached for the sheet of paper. Instantly, she drew it behind her and stepped back out of range.

"Not so fast, buster. What do you mean, you thought I ran?"

Steve hooked his fingers in the waistband of his slacks as he met her stubborn eyes. "I was downstairs having a look around the boyfriend's empty apartment. When I came back upstairs, you were gone. What was I supposed to think? I figured you either ran away or someone took you away. Where were you?"

Emotions flashed across her features. He could see she didn't know whether to be angry at his veiled accusation, or pleased that he'd been worried about her.

"Lynn—"

"How did you get in if Kevin wasn't home? And what do you mean, empty?"

"He's gone, Lynn. Where'd you go?"

"I went downstairs and got Kevin's apartment number from his mailbox. Then I went looking for you. How did you get inside his place?"

He scratched his forehead and then pulled on his beard. He was going to have to do something about this beard. It was starting to bug him. Almost as much as his sexy gray-eyed neighbor.

"I'm a private investigator," he explained on a sigh. "I must have been on my way up in one elevator as you were going down in the other one. Are you going to show me what you found?"

"Are you going to apologize for thinking I'd run off?"

"No," he said quietly, "I'm not." He extended his hand and waited.

Lynn looked startled. Then her eyes blinked dangerously and her chin came up. "Fine. Maybe you'll apologize after you read this."

It was a small sheet of paper, obviously torn from a pad a person might keep next to a telephone. The script was large and sprawling. Baby-sit, it read, followed by the name Montgomery, and then an address on River Road. Below it, 11:00 was underlined.

Lynn watched him closely. His lips set in a firm line.

"So?" he asked.

"What do you mean, so? So now we know where the baby belongs."

Steve gestured to encompass the apartment. "Maybe, but take a look around you. What do you see?"

Her eyes traced the path his hand had taken.

"Maybe this baby belongs to the Montgomerys and maybe it doesn't. Your sister came looking for you yesterday, very upset. Now you can't find her and someone has given a new meaning to the words *spring-cleaning*. Not to mention Kevin."

"What about Kevin?"

"He skipped. Completely. He packed up all his possessions and moved out."

"Moved out?"

"Lock, stock and barrel, as they say. And we still need to call the police."

The baby started to fuss again. Lynn bent down to lift the child. "No," she said firmly. "Not yet. First, we need to go to this address and find out if the baby belongs there."

"Lynn," he began gently.

Her changeable gray eyes reminded him of a storm at sea on a winter's morning. Whatever else she might be, Jerrilynn Rothmore was fiercely loyal to those she cared about.

"I agree, my sister is a ditz. Wasn't that what you called her?"

"An airhead," he corrected.

She rocked the baby tenderly in her arms and averted her gaze. "Same difference. I hate to admit it, but it would be just like Marcy to agree to baby-sit for someone, then be invited somewhere special and decide to bring the baby to me to watch so she could go wherever it was. This break-in could be robbery, pure and simple, and completely coincidental."

He stroked his beard in annoyance. "Do you honestly believe that?" He pinned her with his gaze.

"No," she responded more softly. "All I'm asking is that we go to this address and find out if the baby belongs there. Then we can call the police."

"And what if she does? What if she was kidnapped? We could be arrested."

Lynn stubbornly shook her head. "Marcy did not kidnap this baby."

"Okay, fine. What about this?" he asked, gesturing toward the room in general.

"What about it?"

"Do you plan to leave the door wide open for the next person to walk in and discover it?"

"Couldn't we just lock the door until we come back?"

He shook his head. "The lock is sprung, Lynn. Whoever forced it didn't figure neatness counted a whole lot. We'd have to replace the entire mechanism."

"Oh. Well. We'll just close it. After all, no one can do any more damage, right?" She looked at him hopefully. Then her face took on a distressed look that reached down and grabbed his soul.

He had an irrational desire to protect this woman. Looking at her upturned face, he told himself she was too prim, too intimidating, and she didn't have red hair. He should call the cops and be done with this mess. Still, she was causing emotions to surface in him he hadn't suspected were even part of his nature.

"Please, couldn't we just take a quick drive and find out about the baby first? I promise, we'll call the police after that."

There were at least twenty good reasons to rebuff her request. But Steve met the entreaty in her eyes and tucked every one of those reasons back in place. He had known this woman was going to be trouble. He knew it the day she had moved in.

"Lynn, has it dawned on you that if Marcy was supposed to baby-sit, there might not be anyone at this address?"

From her immediate consternation, it obviously hadn't occurred to her. As always, she rallied quickly. "Maybe not, but it's worth a try. Please?"

Trouble with a capital *T*. He was going to regret this. He just knew it.

Chapter Three

"You were right, the bird went back to her flat. She's got some big chap with her."

"But does she have the babe?"

"Yes. They just came out."

"Follow them. You have to get that baby."

"What about them?"

The silence was heavy with sarcasm. "What do you think?" He placed his hand over his side and rubbed gently. Visions of incarceration skittered through his mind. There was a muttered imprecation in his ear.

"Righto, I'll try to snatch the tyke."

The red-haired man replaced the receiver and rubbed his side. It throbbed horribly. The cut had bled an amazing amount and it continued to seep even now. He knew he needed sutures, but there was nothing he could do about that, just as there was nothing he could do about his partner for the moment. The fellow had been a poor choice, but then, one couldn't always select an accomplice at leisure.

And now the girl had a companion? Who else had she talked to? He was pretty certain the authorities hadn't been alerted yet. But why not? Why hadn't the girl reported what she'd seen?

Acid burned his stomach like the fire licking at his side. Damn that knife. He wasn't sure, but he thought the wound might be getting infected. How had it all gone so wrong?

IT WAS A NICE HOUSE, much classier than its smaller neighbors. It nestled back away from the road, hidden from prying eyes by large fir trees and a thick hedge bordering the property.

The inlaid front door went unanswered. "No one's home," Lynn said needlessly. At least no one had answered the doorbell or their repeated knocks.

"Wait here," Steve told her.

She frowned and shook her head. "I don't think so."

"I love an obedient woman," he muttered.

"Probably why you're still single."

"I don't see any ring on your finger, either."

Lynn glared and Steve had to work to keep his lips from twitching as he walked around the side of the house. There was a breezeway between the two-car garage and the house. "Would you consider knocking on this door for a minute?" he asked, mock-humble.

"Since you asked so politely, how can I refuse?" She strode over and pounded on the door, jarring the sleeping baby, who roused in grumpy protest.

Steve ambled over to the garage door.

"What are you doing?" Lynn shifted the carrier to her other hand.

"I'm going to have a look inside."

She watched intently as he selected a tool from a small leather case he extracted from his pocket and picked the lock. "I've never seen anyone do that except on television."

Steve ignored her. A year-old powder blue Lincoln sat on the concrete floor. Other than that, the garage was empty, aside from a few garden tools.

"Well, that was helpful. We'll not only get arrested for kidnapping, but for breaking and entering a garage, of all things."

He paused to give Lynn a withering look before continuing around the house. She trailed him as he cut across the patio that fanned out around a kidney-shaped pool. He stopped to study the back of the house.

"Nice pool," Lynn said. "Too bad there's no one in it."

For just a moment, Steve pictured Lynn in a skimpy two-piece suit leaning back on a chaise lounge and smiling invitingly.

"Something wrong?"

He was tempted to tell her.

After a moment's hesitation, he decided to take a chance on tripping an alarm. The police would almost be welcome at this point. In fact, he should have followed his instincts and called them from Marcy's apartment, no matter what Lynn wanted to do. He tugged on the nearest sliding glass door. It was locked, but no alarm went off. He wiped away his fingerprints and moved on.

"Be careful," Lynn cautioned. "They probably have an alarm system."

"You think so?" He kept his expression deadpan. Lynn stuck out her tongue at him. The childish gesture made him think of some highly unchildlike responses, but now was not the time.

"Don't worry, if it's a silent alarm, the police are already on their way."

Without waiting for her response, Steve walked between the chairs and an umbrella table to try the French doors leading to the dining room. It surprised the hell out of him when the knob turned easily in his hand.

Steve cursed. "Stay here," he commanded. Lynn looked up from the fussy baby. "If anything happens, get the baby in the car and take off."

Her mouth opened, but something in his expression must have warned her not to argue this time. She gave a jerky nod and began jiggling the carrier in an effort to quiet the baby.

"Hello. Anyone home?" he called into the house. It was silent. An empty, ominous silence. His skin tingled with a sense of danger. There was a fetid smell in the air, like rotting garbage—or a rotting corpse? He should turn around right now and get the hell out of here. This was a mistake. He just knew it.

"Hello?" He stepped inside with caution, noting the expensive Queen Anne furniture. The house was scrupulously neat, a perfect showcase. He moved quickly to his left in the direction of the bedrooms, going rapidly from room to room.

There were five bedrooms, one of which was a den and office. Another, he discovered, was a brightly appointed nursery. It wasn't until he reached the master bedroom that he slowed his pace. An eight-by-ten framed picture held a place of honor on the large triple dresser. A laughing young couple were caught in the blink of the camera's lens as they relaxed on a tropical beach somewhere. Honeymoon?

Steve took a moment to commit both faces to memory without touching the silver frame. With his foot, he nudged open the door to the walk-in closet. Men's and women's clothing hung from the bars, but there were a lot of empty hangers, mostly on the man's side. There was also a spot where suitcases might have sat.

Steve tugged on his beard. He didn't believe for a moment that the couple in the picture had left such a beautiful infant in the care of Lynn's sister and just gone away.

"Steve? Is anyone home?"

Lynn's voice nearly gave him a heart attack. The woman couldn't take an order, to save her life. She stood in the open door to the dining room, patting the fussy baby, now in her arms. The car seat sat on the dining room table.

"She's hungry and wet. Is anyone home?"

"No," he snarled.

"Well, you don't have to bite my head off. Is this her house?"

Steve sighed. "Why don't you ask her? Maybe the baby can identify her bedroom."

"Why are you being so nasty?"

Good question. His body was flooded with adrenaline, and he had nothing to expend it on except her. Not very fair, Gregory. "In case it's escaped your notice, we're in this house without an invitation. If the owners come home, we can be arrested for illegal entry," he said mildly.

"Don't be absurd. We aren't going to do anything illegal." She scowled at him. "At least I'm not."

Mentally, he tried counting to ten. "Listen, Jerrilynn, something is wrong here."

"What?" she demanded, putting the baby against her shoulder in an effort to soothe its cries.

"I don't know, damn it."

She sent him a scathing look. ''Well, while you figure it out, this baby is soaking wet and I need to change her.''

''You can't do that in here,'' he replied flatly.

''Why not?''

It had been his experience that logic seldom worked on members of the opposite sex, but there was always a first time. ''Lynn, there's no one home.''

''So? What do you want me to do, change her on the patio? If there's no one home to ask, then there's no one to tell me I can't come in and change her. I won't disturb anything.''

''Are you crazy? You can't just march in here and make yourself at home.''

''I have no intention of 'making myself at home.' All I want to do is change a diaper and a sleeper.''

''Fine. Do it outside.''

Steve wasn't sure how it happened, but he was standing within a few feet of her. A strand of her glossy brown hair teased the corner of her mouth. If it hadn't been for the dangerous glint in her eyes, he would have reached out and stroked it back into place. ''We don't want to leave fingerprints,'' he explained reasonably.

Her mouth sagged open in utter shock. ''Fingerprints? You're worrying about fingerprints? Why?''

Had any woman ever provoked him so completely with so little effort? He balled his fingers into tight fists in an effort to keep them at his sides, because if he touched her right now he'd either throttle her or kiss her until they were both senseless.

''Because we don't know what the hell is going on here. Now, go back to the car.''

Her features tightened. ''Or what?''

"Or you go use the baby's changing table while I call the police."

She measured the seriousness of his threat. "You'd do it, too."

"Damn straight. It's what I should have done the moment your sister handed me that baby. We have no business in this house," he lectured. "If we're caught here—if someone even suggests we were inside—I'll lose my license. Now, if you can't do exactly as I say, we're leaving and that baby can scream her head off all the way to the police station. Do I make myself clear?"

Lynn pursed her lips. "What did you find?"

Exasperated, he kept his fingers clenched at his sides. He was still too tempted to use them around her pretty little neck. "A big empty house, so far."

"But there is a baby's room?" she persisted.

"Yes."

Their eyes clashed. Steve had a right to be upset and Lynn knew it. If Marcy had agreed to baby-sit for the Montgomerys, she would have come to Lynn armed with clothing and bottles and whatever else was needed. Also, her sister should have called by now to apologize.

Why hadn't she called?

Steve was worried about fingerprints because he still believed this was a kidnapping. Lynn knew Marcy would never do anything so horrible, but it didn't take much to bring Kevin's face into focus. If Kevin was a petty thief, as she suspected, how far a leap was it from stealing jewelry to stealing a baby? But if the child was stolen, where were the parents? Shouldn't they be here, frantically worried about the whereabouts of their beautiful little baby?

"Sorry. You're right."

For just a moment, Steve looked stunned by her acquiescence. Then the business side of him took over again. "Did you touch anything? The door? A chair? The table? Any of the lawn chairs?"

"No. Nothing. I'll wait for you in the car. What are you going to do?"

He straightened his fingers at his sides and relaxed. "I'm going to prowl around for a few minutes. Maybe I can find something that will tell us if this baby is the one who belongs here."

Unhappily, Lynn set the infant in the carrier and retreated through the open door. "You know, Steve, no mother would willingly go off and leave a baby with an unknown sitter for this length of time."

His face was somber. A funny, half-wistful feeling filled him when he looked at the baby. "Go get her changed and fed," he urged gently. "I'll be right out."

Steve headed back down the hall, sharing Lynn's unease.

The baby's room was filled with color. Painted balloons dotted one wall, while a balloon mobile hung over the crib. A balloon night-light sat on the small dresser. Next to that was a silver-framed picture. He took a moment to study the picture and smiled in satisfaction.

"So this *is* her house. I wonder what her name is? And where her mother is," he added in growing concern. A woman who went to such lengths to decorate for her child certainly wouldn't willingly walk away from her.

He entered the converted den across the hall. It was every bit as neat as the other rooms of the house. There were bills and a few other loose papers sitting in tidy piles on top of a broad mahogany desk. Steve shifted a few things carefully before his eyes lit on one of the documents he'd been looking for.

According to the hospital certificate, the baby's name was Rachel Kathleen Montgomery. She'd been born three weeks and two days earlier at Sibley Memorial Hospital to Barrett and Alice Montgomery. There was nothing else of interest on top of the desk, and nothing to indicate the couple had been planning a trip anywhere.

Feeling more edgy by the second, he decided against further prying. He'd already been inside the house a lot longer than he should have. The front hall, living room and the kitchen were the only rooms he hadn't checked yet.

He should have checked the kitchen first.

He entered from the hall and stopped dead, skidding slightly. He looked down and then around. He had found the source of the fetid smell.

"Damn."

Traces of spilled flour littered the floor. Traces that very clearly accepted the imprint of his size-twelve shoes. And his weren't the only prints on the floor. The others, however, were indecipherable, scuffed over. An overturned bag of flour lay on its side, half off the counter. Vegetables rotted on the other side, a fat lazy fly hovering greedily above them. The smell was ripe and strong. But what caught and held his attention were the rusty red and brown stains that spread across the countertop and formed splattered patterns against the pristine shine of the bright white tile floor.

His eyes followed the trail of dried blood to land on a long-bladed knife. It had bounced against the stove and hit the baseboard before coming to rest on the floor beneath the table. A table that was partially set for two.

Steve expelled a sequence of oaths, each more condemning than the first. Blood was clearly visible on the knife as well as the far wall. A bloody dish towel lay wadded in the sink. By stepping unawares into the kitchen and into the path of the fallen flour, he had disturbed possible evidence at the scene of a crime.

The loud trill of the telephone serrated his stretched nerves and made him jump. He glared accusingly at the instrument and the answering machine that perched on a shelf next to it.

"You have reached 555-7492. Please leave your message after the tone." It was a woman's voice, low and throaty. A man's clipped, but well-modulated British tone followed the beep.

"Mrs. Montgomery, this is Bob Haskell. I don't like leaving you a message this way, but I have rung you several times now without being able to reach you. Please telephone me at your earliest convenience. Your husband will be fine, but he was injured in a motorcar accident. My telephone number is area code 703, 555-2487, and my office number is area code 202, 555-6603. Feel free to call no matter what hour you may arrive home. Thank you."

Steve pulled a small notebook from his hip pocket to jot down the two numbers. He was putting it away when he saw the woman. She was tall and slender, wearing jeans and a faded work shirt and carrying a pail brimming with cleaning utensils. Logic told him she wasn't Mrs. Montgomery. Apparently, she had come from a hidden gate in the hedge behind one of the large pine trees. She was striding toward the kitchen patio door and she was staring right at him.

No matter what he said by way of explanation, he could practically kiss his license goodbye once the police arrived. It was illegal entry no matter how you looked at it. Only a fool would believe this wasn't a police matter now.

He scuffed at the flour to obliterate his tracks. Then he stepped over the rest of the flour while his heart lodged against the back of his throat. His mind raced with possible explanations as he went outside to meet the approaching cleaning woman.

The garage would block Lynn's view of the woman. It would also, thankfully, block the woman's view of Lynn and the baby. He was glad he could no longer hear the infant crying. The woman stopped uncertainly at the far edge of the patio. Steve plastered what he hoped was a polite smile on his face and started forward.

"Excuse me, do you work here?"

She nodded without speaking.

"Can you tell me where Mrs. Montgomery is? We were supposed to meet today, but she didn't answer her door. When I came around, I found the patio door unlocked, but she's apparently not home. There's a bit of a mess in her kitchen and I was wondering if she'd had an accident."

The woman took a step back. "I know nothing. I forget my soap." She whirled and began to hurry back the way she had come in a lurching manner, the pail swinging madly against her leg.

"Hey! Wait a minute!" he called, but at the sound of his voice she dropped the pail and began to run in earnest. What the heck had he done to provoke that reaction? he wondered. And then he didn't waste any more time on it. He sprinted in the opposite direction, heading for the car.

Lynn looked up, startled, as he flew around the corner of the house. "What's the matter?" She started to climb out from behind the steering wheel, but he waved her back.

"Go!" he commanded. "Get us out of here. Move!"

He wrenched open the back passenger door and slid inside. "Hurry, damn it! The cleaning woman caught me inside! She ran next door. She'll probably call the police."

Lynn's eyes widened farther, but she automatically responded to his orders. She clicked the seat belt into place and started the engine. As she backed the car down the driveway, she said, "We were going to go to the police anyhow."

"Yeah," he answered, his hands automatically finding the bottle and offering the nipple to the baby. Rachel's carrier was now fastened into the front passenger seat. At any other time, Steve would be amused by Lynn's ploy to keep him from sitting next to her.

"The situation has changed dramatically. There's dried blood and a knife in the kitchen."

"Oh, my God." The air Lynn sucked into her lungs didn't seem to help. Her head whirled with horrible possibilities.

"Precisely. There wasn't a lot of blood. It doesn't mean anyone's been murdered," he tried to assure her, or maybe himself, "but in a situation like this, we have to assume the worst."

She tried to slow her breathing, but she couldn't slow the chills racing up and down her spine. "What are we going to do?" It came out barely a whisper.

His hand rested on her arm. "We're going to go to your apartment and see if your sister left any messages. Then we'll take it from there. Okay?"

"Okay." She tried for a smile that didn't quite make it.

"It's all clear on my side," he told her. Her eyes turned that way, anyhow. As she pulled out into traffic, he told her about the phone message he'd heard.

"Maybe that explains the whole thing. Maybe the mother cut herself and had to go to the hospital. Maybe Marcy was just taking care of the baby until Mrs. Montgomery's husband arrived. Only, he never did."

"Possible."

"Of course it is," she said quickly. "It makes perfect sense."

"Except that whatever took place in that kitchen happened yesterday. Even if Rachel's mother had cut off her finger—and there wasn't *that* much blood—where is the woman today? Why hasn't anyone come looking for Rachel?"

"Rachel?"

"Rachel Kathleen Montgomery."

Lynn felt her face soften. "That's nice. I like it."

His lips turned up at the corners. "So do I." He looked down at the child, feeling protective. "Maybe we'd better stop at the grocery store before we go to the apartment. This bottle is almost empty and we need to stop and pick up some supplies. I think this was our last bottle."

"There's still one in the diaper bag, but okay." She pulled up in front of their local store and Steve also climbed out. "I can get the stuff. You don't have to come with me."

"I do if we want dinner tonight. Do you like steak or are you a vegetarian?"

We? Her heart pounded a little faster as they regarded each other steadily over the hood of the car. Lynn realized that he was asking her to have dinner with him. She had to refuse, of course. She couldn't possibly eat dinner with such a sexy, disturbing man. Having made that decision, she was astonished to hear herself say, "Oh, I watch my fat intake like everyone else, but I love an occasional thick, juicy steak."

His grin flashed dangerously from behind the beard.

Lynn lowered her voice. "Don't let it get around, but I even like sour cream and butter on my baked potato."

"Heresy." His chuckle sent another dangerous current of awareness through her. "Not a complete yuppie, yet, huh?"

"When did they make yuppie a swearword?"

"Probably right after it came into existence. How does broccoli sound?"

"Like a disease, but I happen to love it. I'll grab that and maybe some fruit to make a salad while you get the steaks. We can meet in the baby-food aisle."

His brown eyes twinkled and she felt a wash of color move up her face. As they entered the store, he gave her a jaunty salute and strode off with a handbasket.

The man had a devastating effect on her hormones.

Lynn laid the baby carrier in the bottom of a cart. Rachel Kathleen didn't look unhappy now and it was so nice to have a name to call her by. She was such a beautiful baby. Lynn had always wanted children. What must it be like to give life to a new human being? she wondered.

In the produce aisle, as she reached for a bunch of fresh broccoli, her skin began to prickle. She stopped and glanced around. The sensation that she was being observed was almost overwhelming. Several people shopped nearby, but no one seemed interested in her. Still, the perception skittered along her nerve endings, refusing to go away.

She picked up the broccoli and selected several fruits at random, turning her head frequently to survey the people around her. A woman, the man behind her, and a young boy seemed to inch closer as they studied the grapes. Intuition propelled Lynn away from the fruit and vegetable section. She felt silly, but she also felt hunted. She cast a glance over her shoulder. The man stood alone, looking right at her.

She nearly collided with Steve as he turned down the aisle she had rushed up.

"So this is what they really mean by women drivers," he teased. His expression changed instantly when he took a good look at her face. "What's wrong?"

His presence alone soothed her jangled nerves. She had known him for less than twenty-four hours, yet she trusted him. It was really ironic, since this was the neighbor she hadn't liked at all on first meeting. The neighbor who made her do silly things like get her key stuck in the door when he flashed her that high-wattage smile or drop her mail at his feet at the sound of his soft hello or plow into him with a supermarket cart in an instinctive rush to his side and safety.

Her reaction certainly couldn't be because she found him attractive. She didn't even like men in beards. Yet he seemed to occupy a lot of her thoughts lately, even before the baby had come along. As much as she hated to admit it, in the brief time she'd known him, he'd made an impression. Small details like the way his jeans were worn at the knees, or the way he always checked up and down the hall before opening his door.

Steve had always disturbed her on some level she didn't want to study too closely. It was just that she was finally taking the time to get to know him a bit better, she told herself. That was all. It had nothing to do with the fact that he wasn't living hand-to-mouth as she had suspected when they'd first met. Besides, he was an investigator and therefore someone she could rely on in this situation. That was the only rational explanation. The alternative was too unsettling to contemplate.

"What happened, Lynn?"

Jarred back to the present, she glanced down at the baby. "Nothing—exactly."

"Lynn..."

"I just had the crazy feeling that someone was watching me. There was a man in the produce department—"

"What did he look like?" That same metamorphosis she had seen outside Marcy's door transformed him once again into a dangerous man of action.

"It's okay. I overreacted. I'm a little jumpy right now."

He frowned, even as his eyes scanned the end of the aisle.

"He didn't do anything, really. All he did was look at me. In fact, he may have been with some woman and a young boy. I just felt—uneasy." And that was true. She didn't even know that the man was the cause of her unease. "He was ordinary. I wouldn't be able to describe him."

"Are you sure?"

Was she? The feeling had been so strong. But she didn't want Steve to accost some poor shopper just because she was nervous. "I'm sure."

Steve studied her face, a frown line marring his forehead. "Come on, let's get the baby items and get out of here."

They finished their shopping quickly. Lynn did wonder, but refrained from asking, why they were buying so much formula and so many diapers if they were planning to turn the baby over to the authorities that afternoon. She watched the play of his leg muscles as he hefted an entire case of premixed formula and transferred it to the bottom of her cart. Where was this awareness coming from? She shouldn't even be noticing the fit of his jeans.

Steve's eyes relentlessly scrutinized every person at the checkout counters and surrounding areas as she rummaged through her purse for her wallet to pay for their purchases.

"Hey, wait. Let me get that."

"Don't worry about it," she told him as she extracted her wallet. "It's as good a way as any to use my per diem."

He tilted his head slightly. "Per diem?"

"I am supposed to be in San Francisco at a meeting, even as we speak, only the airline screwed up and couldn't find my reservation. The flight was overbooked, and waiting for the next one would have brought me in too late to attend my segment of the meeting. That's why I'm home."

"Did Marcy know you were going out of town?"

Lynn paid the clerk, accepted her change and put away her wallet. "I understand what you're asking, but you have to know Marcy. I can tell her something one minute and she'll forget the next unless it relates directly to her needs or wants.''

Steve frowned. Lynn spared him a glance and was amazed once again to see how comfortable he looked holding the infant carrier. He looked like a father.

What would Rachel Kathleen look like if she belonged to them instead of the Montgomerys? Would she have dark eyes like Steve's or gray ones like her own? Certainly the baby's hair would be darker and she'd probably be bigger. Steve was an imposing man.

''Would you like to drive?'' she offered quickly, shocked by the direction of her thoughts.

His eyebrows arched in wonder. ''You'd let me behind the wheel of your precious car?''

''Good point. I don't know what I was thinking.''

They shared a grin.

''It's the lack of sleep,'' he told her.

''No doubt.'' She dangled the keys and he took them from her fingers. She felt his brief touch clear to her toes.

''I've never driven an Acura before.''

''I should have asked first. Are you sure you can handle a real car? It will be quite a challenge after that battered old truck you ramble around in.''

He reached out to tap her on the nose. ''I,'' he told her in a voice as smooth as warm butter, ''can handle just about anything you care to throw my way.''

There was no mistaking the devilish twinkle in his eyes. Lynn felt her face heat. Her gaze dropped to his mouth as she wondered what his kiss would be like. Passionate, she decided. Steve wouldn't do anything by half measures.

''Go get the car,'' she said. ''Rachel and I will wait here for you.''

He set the infant seat back in the bottom of the cart. "Okay."

She watched as he jogged across the parking lot. The man even jogged sexy. She was so distracted by her thoughts of him that the green-and-white car that screeched to a halt in front of her came as a complete surprise.

A burly, dark-haired man leapt from the vehicle. It was the man from the produce department. Instinctively, Lynn pushed the shopping cart behind her. Fear lodged in her throat as he raced around his car toward her.

A horn squalled in the parking lot. Lynn spared a glance in that direction. Steve was running back toward her. He'd never make it in time.

The stranger lunged at the cart. Lynn brought her leg up in a roundhouse kick. Amazingly, the kick connected, jolting her backward against the cart. Rachel began to cry.

It had been years since Lynn had taken the course in self-defense. She had forgotten a lot. The one thing she remembered was the instructor telling them to always take the offensive when they could.

Lynn screamed out a war cry and swung her purse with all her strength. The bag caught her attacker in the side of the face. She followed up with a kick to his groin. The man staggered. Someone yelled. Lynn spotted the tall, rangy grocery store manager barreling in their direction. Rachel's cries mounted in volume.

Hunched, the attacker backed away. He knocked against an empty cart, fumbled for the door of his car and scrambled inside. He was gone in seconds. Lynn was starting to shake as Steve reached the scene. Onlookers pooled, murmuring in dismay.

"Are you okay?" Steve said, panting.

The manager voiced almost the same words.

"Let's get out of here." Steve took her arm.

"Come on inside," the manager insisted. "My assistant is calling the police."

Steve remembered the cleaning woman at the Montgomery house and the footprints he no doubt had tracked over the carpeting. Calling the police no longer seemed like a good idea.

As though reading his thoughts, Lynn shook her head. "No," she told the manager. "I need to take the baby home. We'll call the police from there."

"Could we have your name so the police can contact you?" Steve added quickly. "You could also collect the names of the other witnesses for them." He turned to look at the gathered throng. "Did anyone get the license number of that car?"

No one had. Steve disentangled them from the scene by snatching the carrier holding the crying baby, and taking Lynn by one arm. He hustled them out to the parking lot and into the car. Then he drove back to grab the groceries and stuff them into the trunk.

"Oh, God," she breathed out in a soft whoosh of air. "I can't believe that just happened."

"You're incredible."

Her feather gray eyes were impossibly wide. Adrenaline had sent a rosy flush to her cheeks. Steve wanted nothing more than to hug her tight and kiss those soft, full lips, but he probably wouldn't stop there and traffic was much too heavy.

He pulled out into the road. "Where'd you learn to kick like that?"

He heard her shaky laugh, but her comeback was quick and certain. "Overly amorous boyfriends."

Steve grinned in appreciation, even as she twisted around to check on Rachel.

"She can't be hurt," Lynn protested. "I jerked the cart away when I realized that man's intention."

Steve braked for a stoplight and reached over the seat to stroke the baby's cheek. "Don't worry. I'm sure she's fine. She probably just wants some attention." Even as he said the words, Rachel's cries softened, becoming less pronounced.

"See?"

Lynn settled back against the seat, feeling more upset now that everything was over. "Steve, what's going on?"

He hesitated for so long, she didn't think he was going to answer. At a red light, he twisted around to study her.

"I don't know. Absolutely nothing adds up. I'd give a lot to talk to your sister right now. I'd like to know what she was doing with the baby in the first place."

The light changed and traffic started moving again. He drove with easy confidence on the crowded streets. It was the looks he kept darting in the rearview mirror that bothered Lynn.

"Is someone following us?" she asked fearfully.

"I can't tell."

"That isn't reassuring."

"Sorry." He drove aimlessly for a few minutes, still eyeing the mirror, before pulling into their apartment parking lot.

"Are you going to lose your license because that woman saw you back at the house?"

He shut off the engine before answering her. "I hope not. But I would have stood a better chance if I had stayed and called the police from there."

"Well, why didn't you?"

His gaze didn't waver. "I'm not sure."

That was true. It certainly hadn't been for Marcy's sake. What little he knew of Lynn's sister, he didn't like. And it couldn't be because of Lynn herself. She aggravated the hell out of him.

Whatever muse was motivating him wasn't leaving explanations behind. He grabbed the bags with the perishables and followed Lynn inside to the elevators.

They rode up, then stepped off the elevator and started down the hall. Steve came to an abrupt stop. Lynn's eyes followed his. Even from where they stood, they could plainly see her door standing ajar.

He dropped the two brown sacks of groceries and grabbed her arm when she would have started forward. A quick, hard shake of his head stopped the words that had formed on her lips. He nodded toward his door, instead. She argued with a look and a constricted expression. His gaze traveled pointedly from the child in her arms to her front door and back again. She conceded with a nod.

Steve slid his keys from his pocket and unlocked his door, but his gaze never wavered from the partially open door next to it. He propelled Lynn and the baby inside his apartment and raced for his bedroom. The gun was a cold heavy weight in the palm of his hand, but the metal was some comfort as he started back out into the hall. Lynn's gray eyes fastened on the weapon.

"Steve," she protested in a whisper, "it could be Marcy."

He nodded but he didn't break stride. "I hope it is," he told her. "Don't worry. It's tempting, but I won't shoot her. Wait here and stay inside."

Mindful of his tumble the last time he tried going through a door like this, Steve went in low, but not so fast. It was a wise choice. The wrecking crew had been busy. The devastation wasn't as thorough as at Marcy's apartment, but little had been overlooked.

Inside Lynn's bedroom, Steve stared at the filmy lingerie at his feet. Seeing Marcy's underwear tossed around her bedroom hadn't fazed him. Lynn's pair of mint green panties lying near his shoe sent a flush of cold rage through him. He bent down and lifted the wisp of material and set it on the bed. The situation was no longer impersonal. Lynn would feel violated when she saw this. He wished there was some way to spare her.

When he turned around, he saw her standing in the living room. Her wounded eyes were taking in the damage, the knuckles of her right hand pressed to her trembling lips.

"What are you doing in here?" he said. Without pausing for breath, he asked, "Where's the baby?"

"On the floor of your bedroom."

He sped past her without a word. Rachel lay blissfully asleep in the carrier exactly where Lynn had left her. She ran into his back when he came to a halt in his bedroom doorway. She closed stricken eyes and swayed.

"I didn't think. I was afraid. When you took the gun..."

His hands steadied her and he led her back to the living room and a dilapidated chair. "I know. You have to trust me, Jerrilynn. I wouldn't have shot your sister—even though she has landed us smack in the middle of one hell of a mess."

Lynn seemed fragile in that moment, sitting in his dumpy wing chair. For the first time, he wished he had bothered getting decent furniture so she would have something more comfortable to sit on.

"I'm sorry about your apartment," he told her softly. "We're going to have to go back over there so you can look around. I need to know if anything is missing. Then we call the police. No more stalling."

She nodded mutely.

"We can't afford to leave the baby alone even for a minute, agreed?"

She pushed herself up and out of the chair. A gutsy lady, he thought in approval.

"Agreed. I know we have to call the police, but if you're a private detective like you said, then I want to hire you."

He stared at her in surprise. "To do what?"

"I want you to find my sister."

"Lynn..."

"Then you can testify at my murder trial."

"What?"

"My sister. I'm going to kill her with my bare hands when we find her."

Chapter Four

She stared at the wreckage of her parents' living room and swallowed hard. Life had become a nightmare from which she couldn't wake up. The pills that usually created a euphoric world weren't working at all now.

A shard of broken vase crunched under her shoes. She looked down. It had been one of her mother's favorites. A tear tracked a familiar path down her pale cheek, but a sudden sound from overhead riveted her to the floor, one hand frozen in the act of wiping at the moisture. She wasn't alone in the house.

Panic threatened to send her screaming. Self-preservation held her very still. Instantly, her mind pictured pale blue eyes as they watched her through the kitchen window. A tiny whimper escaped her lips. The murderer was in her parents' house.

Heavy footsteps crossed the floor above her, heading for the stairs. There was no time to debate a course of action. Her car sat in the driveway. He would know she was here. She had to run.

A kitchen pan skittered across the floor as she crashed through debris to reach the back door. She knew she'd never make it, but she had to at least try.

CARRYING THE SLEEPING baby in the car seat, Steve and Lynn returned to her apartment to survey the damage. Someone was extremely angry. Was this anger directed at Lynn because of the baby? He saw her tense features and his fingers knotted in tight fists as he prowled the wreckage.

Steve hunted for the telephone. Almost everyone had an answering system these days and Jerrilynn was no exception.

"A common answering machine?" he teased. The red light blinked merrily. "I thought for sure you'd have voice mail or a fancy computer for E-mail."

His teasing had the desired effect. Some of the tension left her features. "Sorry to disappoint you. My computer's being upgraded. I have to make do for now."

She hurried past him and depressed the switch. A man's hearty voice issued forth.

"Hello, Lynn, it's David." Lynn cringed. "Sorry I missed you before you left again. Hope California has better weather than Orlando. It's raining buckets down here. I'm up to my eyeballs in work and we're a little behind, so I probably won't get in until late Friday night instead of Thursday. Did I remember to tell you that Valerie and Irwin are having a small bash Saturday night?"

He saw the nails of her right hand embed themselves in the back of the nearest chair. Obviously, this news ranked right up there with root canals and dropped transmissions.

"I know you aren't real fond of them," David's voice continued cheerfully, "and it is last-minute, but she's a client, I'm afraid. Mr. Bradshaw was invited and inside information has it that he's going to show.

That being the case, I absolutely must put in an appearance. I hope you didn't have other plans again."

Because he was watching her expression so closely, he saw her face tighten in a flash of anger and then her eyes flickered closed.

"I'll try to call you to confirm when I get in, if it isn't too late. Oh, and I'd really appreciate it if you'd wear your blue dress instead of the black silk. Mr. Bradshaw is a bit—conservative. The black dress is, well, rather low-cut for Mr. Bradshaw, dear."

Both hands gripped the back of the chair tight enough to leave marks. Steve didn't blame her a bit. He disliked the man, sight unseen. He also found he wanted very much to see Lynn in the black silk dress.

"If I don't reach you before then, give me a call Saturday afternoon," the oily voice instructed. "We'll take in dinner before we go. A new Italian place just opened that Mr. Bradshaw likes a lot. If we get there before six, the entrées are half-price."

That figured. Let David-the-dork take Mr. Bradshaw and leave Steve to Lynn and the black silk dress.

"Don't work too hard," David continued. "You know how you tend to overdo. Kisses."

Steve wanted to make gagging motions, but Lynn wouldn't meet his eyes. She looked angry and embarrassed, which kept him from making any gesture or comment at all.

The next message was from a woman who wanted to have lunch the following week. Then came the one they'd been hoping for.

"Lynn? Please pick up," a young feminine voice pleaded. The two sisters even sounded alike, Steve decided. "Where are you? Oh, God, you have to be home! I'm in terrible trouble! If they catch me, they'll kill me!"

Marcy spoke in breathless gasps. There was a muffled sob and then the shrill timbre of her voice leveled out. "You always did say I was going to have to grow up and take responsibility for my actions, but oh, sis, I'm in such trouble this time." The voice clogged with tears. "I know what you'd tell me to do, but I can't go to the police and Kevin skipped out and they'll think I was involved, but I wasn't. Not really. I don't know what I'm going to do. Oh, God." There was a long pause and another snuffle.

Lynn's expression was so distressed that Steve slid an arm around her shoulders. She felt fragile beneath his hand, and he could feel her trembling.

"I'll call you later," Marcy finished. "I don't dare go back to your place in case he's watching." There was a click and the mechanical recorder stamped the date and time of the call. They had missed her by less than an hour.

There followed yet another message from a friend who just wanted to chat, but neither Lynn nor Steve listened. He turned Lynn to press her against his shoulder. He held her close for several minutes, stroking her back. She filled his arms perfectly, as if she was made to be held there. When she took a deep breath, he allowed her to step back.

"Okay?"

She gave him a weak smile and a nod. "Why didn't she leave a number where I could reach her? I could just shake her."

"Somehow, I don't think shaking your sister would help. Why don't you take a quick look around and see what's missing."

"Do you think Marcy meant Kevin kidnapped the baby?"

He frowned and absently stroked his beard. "There's no point in second-guessing anything your sister said. She was obviously distraught. But I do wonder how she knows Kevin skipped out. Does she have a key to his place?"

Lynn didn't answer. She rubbed her temples as though she had a headache. She probably did, he thought. Little sister was enough to give anyone a headache. She was a spoiled brat. Lynn had probably been pulling Marcy's problems out of the manure pile on a regular basis.

They were going to have to call the police. Already it would be hard to explain the delay—particularly after the incident at the grocery store. His stomach rumbled right on cue at the thought of food.

"Hey, I don't know about you, but I'm starving."

Lynn looked as if he had sprouted horns. He gave her his best little-boy grin and shrugged. "This mess will wait. I'll run downstairs and bring up the baby stuff and we can go back over to my apartment, make a sandwich and decide how to proceed. How does that sound?"

"I'm not hungry," she told him.

"You only think that now. Once I present you with one of my infamous Dagwood-style sandwiches, you'll change your mind. Come on. I think better on a full stomach."

"How are we going to lock the apartment?"

Steve walked over and studied the door. "Whoever's doing the B and E doesn't know anything about finessing a lock, that's for sure." He motioned her over and pointed at the broken latch. "There's nothing we can do about this.'' Without seeming to, Steve maneuvered Lynn outside and into the hall. ''Wait in my living room. I'll run down and grab the rest of the stuff from the car.''

Lynn let herself be persuaded, mainly because she was so confused that any direction was better than none. She stepped inside Steve's stark living room and sat down in his lumpy wing chair. Only seconds passed before she heard the elevator again. Even for a gung-ho, take-charge guy like Steve, that was fast. Had he forgotten something?

Or maybe it wasn't Steve.

Heart pounding, Lynn peered out through the peephole. Her gasp was a muted whisper of sound. Two uniformed policemen were drawing guns even as she watched.

''Call it in,'' the taller one whispered. ''Looks like we've got a situation.''

The shorter one spoke into a handheld radio, then both men approached her door and disappeared from view. She could hardly breathe. Furtively, she cracked open the door.

''No,'' she heard someone say, ''no sign of the perpetrator or the Rothmore woman.'' There was a burst of static and unrecognizable noise and then, ''Yeah, it looks like the attempted kidnapping wasn't a hoax. You'd better send in the detectives. Somebody's got a lot of explaining to do.'' Another burst of static. ''Okay. Ten-four.''

Lynn scooted back inside, closing the door silently. Steve was going to lose his license and it was all her fault. She grabbed her purse, the diaper bag, then the baby and looked around quickly for anything else she might need. She couldn't see the officers when she cracked open the door, but she could plainly hear them moving around inside her apartment. She had to warn Steve. His door latched behind her noiselessly as she hurried down the hall toward the stairwell.

Her heart thundered in cadence all the way down the steps, her breathing echoing hollowly in her ears. Rachel started to cry again. "Sorry, sweetie. Hang in there. If this costs Steve his license, I'll never forgive Marcy."

The baby was not impressed.

"I should have listened to him. He wanted to report everything right from the beginning. Why didn't I listen to him?"

Steve was just entering the building when she reached the lobby.

"Turn around! Back to the car! Hurry!"

"What's wrong?" But he reversed direction as she sped awkwardly across the floor toward him. The lobby was empty, but there could have been a dozen people standing there. Lynn didn't care, she just wanted to protect this man.

"The police are upstairs. Come on."

"Lynn..." He stopped moving, but she was practically running from the building. He followed at a cumbersome trot, the heavy box of formula and the large bag of diapers clutched in his arms.

She headed toward her parked car. Steve changed direction on her. "My truck is closer." Lynn turned to protest, but he didn't give her a choice. He dumped the boxes in the back of the cab. "Give me Rachel." He climbed into the back seat and fastened the carrier in place. In seconds, he was behind the wheel with the engine running.

"Now, what's going on?"

Lynn pointed. A second police car was pulling up behind the one already parked in front of the building. His heart sank. The cleaning woman must have found the mess at the Montgomery home. A neighbor probably got the plate number.

Steve put the truck in gear, forcing himself to drive normally. He wanted to talk to the police, all right, but on his terms, not theirs.

"What happened?"

"I'm so sorry." Her voice sounded anguished. "They went to my apartment. They said someone was going to have a lot of explaining to do."

"Hell, we knew that. Why didn't you go over and introduce yourself?"

"Because I don't want you to lose your license. What was I supposed to tell them?" Without hurting him. "You wanted to report Rachel right away. I didn't listen."

Lynn had added him to the list of those she protected? Steve found a strange warm glow spread at the idea. It had been a long time since anyone had wanted to protect him from anything. He debated turning around and going back. Explanations would no doubt be awkward, but the longer they delayed, the worse it would get. His stomach rumbled loudly.

"What are you doing?" she asked when he pulled into the parking lot of a pizza parlor. "We have to get out of here."

He shut down the truck and twisted slightly to look at her. "Lynn, I'm hungry. We are going to go inside, have some lunch and discuss how to approach the police."

"Approach them?"

"We can't run forever."

Color returned to her face. "I know that. What if they find us sitting here?"

He pulled the keys from the ignition and opened the door.

"We'll invite them to join us. As long as they wait until after I get something to eat, they'll be welcome. The food is terrible at the police station," he told her.

Lynn clicked her teeth together. While her tension drained at his reaction, her frustration mounted. She didn't understand him at all.

"Trust me."

When he looked at her like that, she wanted nothing more. Where was her common sense? "Yeah. Right."

He grinned that naughty-boy grin that went straight to her core as he leaned over to brush a quick kiss on her lips. The action robbed her of speech. Her lips tingled at the brief contact. She placed a fingertip over them as she watched him undo the car seat.

"Are you coming?"

Somehow, she found herself inside the restaurant squeezed into a back booth. Steve set the carrier on the opposite side, removed the baby and slid in alongside Lynn. The waitress hurried over and began to fuss over Rachel.

Lynn froze. Steve, however, had no qualms about answering the woman's questions or responding to her comments. He sat back, completely relaxed, and talked as though he were the proud father and this was a normal outing. He kept running one hand up and down Lynn's arm in a possessive manner that set off crazy inexplicable shivers.

She was flabbergasted at how natural the falsehoods sounded falling from his lips. Her heart was thundering in her chest, and she kept wondering who to call when the police hauled them off to jail. Steve didn't seem worried. She watched in amazement as he held the waitress in thrall with his charm and humorous stories about parenting. It was unbelievable. He was outrageous. Within minutes, he and the woman were chatting like old friends.

Lynn sat back and tried to relax. What did Steve look like under all that hair on his face? Would he have strong features or a weak, chinless face? Who cared? How could she even be wondering such a thing? It couldn't matter. She wouldn't let it. Only, the absurd thought kept running through her head that Steve would never tell her not to wear the black dress. Steve would probably love that dress.

"Is that okay, sweetheart?"

She stared at him blankly. His smile was tender as he pulled the menu from in front of her. He had a nice smile. She liked the way his eyes crinkled up in the corners when he smiled. Then he turned back to the waitress and winked conspiratorially. "The baby had her up most of the night, last night. I think she's still half-asleep."

"Oh, I remember those days well," the waitress agreed. "Don't you worry, honey. It'll seem like forever right now, but you wait, they grow so fast you won't hardly remember. I'll go put your order in." Off she went with a pleased smile.

He ran the knuckle of his index finger across her cheek, leaving searing heat in its wake. "Close your mouth. Everything's fine."

"Are you crazy?" she asked in a strangled whisper. "That woman thinks we're married and this is our baby."

"Would you care to explain the truth to her?"

"Don't be smart. What are we going to do?"

"Eat lunch as soon as it comes," he responded. Then his expression gentled. "It will be okay, Lynn. Trust me."

Trust him? Why should she? How could she?

Why did she?

As he started to slide out of the booth, panic assailed her anew. "Where are you going?"

Steve bent over and laid a warm hand on her shoulder. His smile was a flash of teeth beneath his beard. "Relax. I'm going to the little daddies' room and then I want to call my office." He set the baby back in her seat and placed it on the table. "Can you sit here a few moments and pretend that everything is wonderful?"

"No, I most certainly—"

This kiss wasn't a quick brush, yet he kissed her as if she was as fragile as spun glass. The tip of his tongue flicked out to trace her lips. Lynn shuddered at the contact. His mouth covered hers then, urgently confident, possessive. The kiss was warm honey, burning its way to her soul, leaving utter devastation in its wake.

"I'll be right back, Jerrilynn. Promise."

Her lips throbbed with the power of that short possession. Speech was beyond her.

Steve left the table and threaded his way across the room, glad his jeans weren't any tighter. He hadn't meant to kiss her. And he certainly hadn't meant for the kiss to leave him so hot and ready for more. Jerrilynn was dangerous. More dangerous than any other woman he had ever known. Did David-the-dork appreciate that fact? Just how serious was their relationship?

It was nearing noon and the restaurant was crowded. He let his gaze drift over faces, studying those near him out of habit. An uneasy feeling still hovered in the back of his mind and he couldn't seem to shake the sensation completely. From the pay phones, he could watch their table, so he would know that Lynn and the baby were safe.

"O'Hearity Investigations," Theresa answered. Either Tim wasn't there or his private line was busy.

"Gregory here, let me talk to Tim."

"Oh, yes, sir. That is, I'll see if he's in. One moment." And she promptly disconnected him. Steve dug for another quarter and muttered under his breath about inept trainees.

"O'Hearity Investigations."

"This is Gregory again and I am down to my last quarter. Don't you dare disconnect me."

There was a tiny gasp and a tremulous voice said, "I'm sorry, sir. Really. It was an accident. I just—"

"Theresa," he said slowly, drawing on every bit of patience he could muster, "just put me through, okay? And don't disconnect me."

"Oh, yes, sir. I mean, no, sir. I won't. He's on another call at the moment. Can you hold on, Mr. Gregory? I'm really sorry, sir. Honest. It won't happen again." And she promptly disconnected him once more.

Steve uttered an oath. He didn't know where Tim had found the girl, but at this point, he was all for sending her back. He could go out to his truck and call from there, but he didn't want to leave Lynn and Rachel alone. No one manned the cash register and Steve had to wait several minutes before he could get change for his ten.

By then, he could see Lynn looking a bit frantic, probably because the waitress was back at their table, hovering. As he drew closer, he realized it was more than just the waitress. Rachel was fussing and fuming in Lynn's arms. Her tiny hands waved in the air.

"Here, honey," he said. "Let me take her for a few minutes."

Her relief was almost palpable.

Lynn handed over the infant and sidled out of the booth, trying not to brush up against him. She hadn't yet shrugged off the effects of that kiss and she wasn't sure she was ready for another dose of his potent masculinity.

"I have to run to the ladies' room. I'll be right back."

Steve watched her go and marveled at the unconscious sway of her hips. She could dress as primly as she wanted. Nothing could hide the provocative, utterly feminine woman beneath her clothes. He gave a mental shake at his wayward thoughts.

Rachel drew his attention and he smiled at the baby. "You know something, kid, that phone call to your house from the very proper British gentleman is a real stumper."

Rachel smiled up at him. "I'm sure glad you're too young to understand what's going on right now."

Was it Rachel's father lying in the hospital or someone else? Were her parents married, divorced, or what? He needed information, preferably before he talked to the police. They were going to have to do that soon. Every minute they delayed was going to have to be explained.

What was taking Lynn so long?

Lynn exited the stall and went over to the sink to wash her hands and splash cold water on her face. The fact was, the baby had kept her up all night and she was tired. Maybe that was why she was going along with things instead of taking charge in her customary manner.

Take charge. Hah. She'd like to see the person who could take charge of Steven Gregory. There was no question about it. That damn sexy man scrambled every one of her mental circuits. That was why she was going along with things.

She heard the door open as she reached for a paper towel. Suddenly, a large, hairy hand clamped over her mouth, preventing the spill of the scream that came shooting upward. Without thought, she lashed her foot backward. She took only momentary satisfaction when her heel connected with the attacker's shin. The grunt it elicited did nothing to loosen his hold. Lynn writhed and twisted in an effort to break free, but he held on with unyielding strength.

"Cut it out, you bloody bitch. I only want the babe. Do you understand? Give me the child." His accent was pronounced, and so was the smell of the horrible cologne he was wearing. Her struggles forced him to drop his hand just enough that she was able to sink her teeth into one finger. She bit down as hard as she could.

Everything happened at once after that. Her captor loosened his hold and yelled. The door rocked open and a heavyset woman entered with two young girls at her side. The woman took one look at the scene, stopped dead and let out a lusty scream. Up came her purse, and she beat at the man, screeching in an awful bellow. The children shrieked and screamed as only children can do.

Lynn twisted free, stumbling backward. Her attacker shoved the woman aside and leapt for the door.

A waitress, starting down the hall to investigate the commotion, sprang back when he charged into her at a full run. Unfortunately, she spun backward into a second waitress carrying a large tray of drinks. Fluid sailed upward as if in slow motion, promptly dousing the startled people waiting in line to be seated. In an attempt to pursue the fleeing man, Lynn tangled with the scattering patrons and suddenly Steve was there.

"Look out," someone yelled. "He's got a gun!"

Who had a gun?

The pandemonium was incredible. People began to push and shove, clogging the entrance in an effort to get out of the way. Yells and screams only added to the confusion. It took Steve a full second to realize that he was the one holding the gun that had sent everyone into hysterics.

His eyes sought Lynn's. "Get Rachel!" Without waiting, he hollered, "Police! Clear the door!"

Lynn didn't have to be told twice. Neither did most of the people who scrambled to get out of his way. She darted back to their table and found the friendly waitress holding the baby, gaping in shock.

"Thanks," Lynn muttered, snatching the baby from her arms and setting Rachel in the carrier. She scooped up the diaper bag and her purse and dashed after Steve.

Steve chased after the squealing car on foot as it raced for the open street. A momentary lull in traffic allowed the driver to pull out onto the road. Cursing, Steve pivoted and ran back to the truck. Lynn was already there with the doors open. She had tossed her purse and the baby bag inside and was fastening the carrier with the back seat belt. Not to be overlooked in all the commotion, the infant cried loudly enough to puncture eardrums.

Moments later, they rocketed onto the street even though Steve knew it was already too late. The Mazda was out of sight, and he had only a partial on the plate number. He gunned the engine, pushing as hard as he dared in the heavy traffic. His eyes scanned the side streets in a desperate effort to determine where his quarry had gone.

"What happened?" he asked as he drove.

Lynn explained. "If that woman hadn't come in when she did—"

"Was he armed? Did he threaten you with anything?"

"No. He just grabbed me and said he wanted the baby. He was British. You couldn't mistake his accent."

He stopped for a red light and turned to look at her. Her eyes were shut, her skin was pasty, and he could see her lower lip trembling. He cursed himself for a fool and pulled into the first parking lot he saw.

She opened her eyes, tears hovering, and looked at him when he turned off the engine.

"Come here."

Her stricken eyes met his for just a moment and then she allowed herself to curl into the warmth of his broad chest. "I'm okay," she told him, but it felt so safe being held in the strength of his arms.

"I know you are," he said against her mouth. "You're more than okay." She reached her hands up to circle his neck. It was all the encouragement he needed.

He took her mouth in a hungry kiss that made her ache. She savored the taste and feel of him. Hard, masculine heat that drew her more deeply into his embrace. She was aware of the soft bristles of his beard against her skin, awed by the muscles she could feel beneath her fingers. His tongue probed for entrance and her lips parted instantly to welcome him.

Suddenly, he drew back, his head twisted toward the back seat.

"The baby," he muttered.

Rachel's cries reached Lynn's fogged brain. The baby was in the carrier facing the back seat, and she was not at all happy with the view.

Lynn shivered, trying to overcome the tumult of emotions that racked her. Under the spell of his lips, she'd forgotten all about the baby.

"Take it easy, kid," Steve said as he unfastened the belt holding the infant in place. "You sure are a demanding little thing. Not unlike some other female I know."

His eyes scored her, much as his lips had done. Heat flamed in her face and he smiled knowingly. "You did great back there," he told her quietly.

His words of praise warmed her. "I did?"

"Oh, yeah. I've worked with professionals who didn't behave as coolly as you did under tight conditions like those."

Pleased, she smiled.

"You did great in here, too," he added. Electricity sizzled in his dark expression.

Lynn drew her fingernail away from her puffy lips and struggled to ignore the heat that suffused her body.

"There wasn't time to be scared. I just reacted."

"You have fantastic reactions."

The cab of the truck was too small. There wasn't enough oxygen for all of them. Desperately, she fastened her gaze on Rachel. "Is she okay?"

His eyes crinkled at the corners. "She's just wet and hungry, as usual," he reassured her. Lynn relaxed.

"Why don't you pull a diaper out of the box and we'll change her. We still have a bottle, don't we?"

"I think so. Aren't we going back?"

Steve shook his head. "Not right now."

"Why not?"

"I'll be in a mess of trouble for that scene back there."

"Why?"

"The police frown on people who pull guns, even people who are licensed to carry them. They also don't like it when a citizen pretends to be a policeman." He shrugged. "It was the only way I could keep a riot from breaking out. I need some answers before I talk to the police."

"But, your license . . ."

"If I lose it, I lose it. I have other plans in the works. It will just mean I have to move up my timetable."

"Other plans?"

He looked up from changing the baby's diaper and flashed her a smile. "You sound like a parrot." At her expression, he reached out and tapped her nose. "Being an investigator is just something I'm doing for now. It pays the bills, but I do have other plans for my life." His voice lowered. "I'll tell you about them someday."

Lynn fought against the intimate spell he weaved. "May I ask you a personal question?"

His eyebrows arched suggestively. "Anything you like."

"Why do you wear that horrible beard?"

Steve reached up to stroke the soft bristles. "Horrible?"

Lynn flushed. "Well, maybe *horrible* is too strong a word, but it gives you a—I don't know—disreputable look?"

His lips twitched. "Disreputable, huh? No one's ever put it quite that way before."

"Is it because you'd look like a yuppie if you shaved it off? I know you consider yuppies lower than dirt."

"Hey, now, I never said that. Lower than grass, certainly, but lower than dirt...?" He held up a hand at the glint in her eyes. "Only teasing. Actually," he went on more seriously, "I needed it for the case I was just working on. My job was to look 'disreputable.'"

She answered the twinkle in his eyes with an open smile. "Congratulations. You're a success story."

Steve chuckled.

"How did you became a private investigator?"

"My friend Tim needed help. I had the background and he knew I was tired of police work."

"You were a policeman?"

"Once upon a time. I didn't care for it much and Tim needed someone to mix with a group of vagrants while he searched for a runaway. Tim can do a lot of things, but he'd never pass for a vagrant. He's a yuppie through and through. You'd like him."

"I'm sure."

His chuckle came again. Even Rachel seemed to be listening as he finished snapping her sleeper into place. "There you go, kid. All clean and dry. Anyhow, I agreed to give it a shot. I haven't had any regrets."

Lynn heard the finality in his answer, so she took the baby from his arms to offer it the nipple of the bottle she had ready. "Where are we going next?"

"Since we didn't get anything to eat back there, I'm still hungry. There's a fast-food place up ahead. Think you can handle that or would you rather try another restaurant?"

She shuddered delicately. "No, thanks. Once was enough. A drive-through sounds wonderful. Then what?"

"Then we have to ditch my truck and find a bolt hole. What's your phone number?"

She blinked and gave it to him. Bolt hole? She was about to ask, when Steve leaned down and depressed the keypad to his car phone. Her answering machine cut in on the fourth ring, and he waited through her message for the beep. He held it without saying a word for several seconds, then he calmly replaced the receiver.

"What did you do that for?"

"I didn't save your messages when I played them at your apartment so the light won't be on, but in case the police decide to play the tape anyhow, that should have erased the other messages."

"I never would have thought of that."

"That's why I'm the detective and you're the client."

"I am?"

"Don't you remember? You plan to kill your sister after I find her. What would you like to eat?"

They postponed further conversation until they were settled in the back corner of the fast-food parking lot, with the car facing out. The greasy odor of French fries and burgers filled the small cab. Rachel seemed content in her carrier in the back seat where they had once again placed her.

"I've been thinking," Lynn said, breaking the comfortable silence.

"Uh-oh."

She ignored that. "I know how to keep you out of this."

Steve swallowed and set his burger down. "Out of what?"

"How about if I go to the police, tell them you brought the baby over to me and I've been running around trying to find my sister ever since? You don't have to be mentioned again at all."

Steve reached for his soft drink. "And how do we explain about the incident in the grocery store, not to mention the one at the pizza parlor?"

"Well, what if I just happened to run into you there?"

His eyebrows rose. "Where?"

"The store."

"And I rushed you away without waiting for the police to come? Not very likely. And that still doesn't get us off the hook at the pizza parlor."

She regarded him thoughtfully, but her expression remained undaunted. "You were just trying to get me away from the source of potential danger?"

"I pulled a gun, Lynn," he reminded her.

"But the man tried to kidnap me."

"I identified myself as a police officer."

"Well, they might be a little miffed about that," she conceded, "but they won't take away your license for it, will they?"

"For that, no. But add to that illegal entry, leaving the scene of a crime and withholding evidence—namely, Rachel—probably."

"But they don't need to know you were in Kevin's apartment, and I'm the one who refused to go to the police until I talked to Marcy." She aimed a French fry in his direction. "They might not be happy with you, but they can't hold you responsible for my actions. You certainly haven't done anything to lose your license over so long as they don't know you were with me at Marcy's apartment or my own. Maybe we're just messy housekeepers."

"You're forgetting, a cleaning woman saw me inside the Montgomery house. Besides, you won't make much of a character witness if you're in jail on a charge of kidnapping."

"I didn't do anything."

"Put yourself in their position. You've got the baby. Let me give my boss another call," he added before she could argue.

Again he tried Tim's direct line. It switched over to the receptionist.

"O'Hearity Investigations."

"Theresa, this is Steve Gregory again." He actually heard her gulp. He cut off her tearful apologies. "Who's in the office right now?"

"No one."

"What do you mean, no one?"

"I'm sorry," she whimpered. "I'm the only one here. They all went out in a hurry. I'm alone." Steve felt as if he had just kicked a puppy.

"Could I take a message?" she asked, sounding fearful.

Did he dare leave one? Did he have a choice? "Theresa, give Tim my message as soon as he comes in. Tell him to call me on my car phone right away. He has the number. Okay?"

"Yes, sir. I promise. Right away."

"Problems?" Lynn asked when he hung up.

"New receptionist," he replied succinctly. "It looks like we're on our own for a little longer."

"So what do we do now?"

"Now we steal a car."

Chapter Five

"Murder! What the hell are you talking about?" he snarled. His thumbs bit into her arms with bruising strength.

"Don't be so stupid." She tried to pull free. "I saw him. That friend of yours. The one you didn't want to introduce me to that day. He and another man killed her. You're going to jail for the rest of your life, you stupid jerk, so let me go." She tried to wrench her arm away, but his grip tightened and his face took on a fearsome expression.

"You're crazy." But his voice lacked conviction. "Lenny wouldn't murder anyone."

She tossed back her mane of hair. "Fat lot you know. I'm telling you I saw them. Your friend said she was dead."

He released her then.

"Why do you think I'm trying to hide?" she continued, her voice shrill. "I thought you were them. When they find me, they're going to kill me, too. We have to hide."

He began to pace the messy kitchen, kicking things aside as he went. A pan and a wooden spoon flew into the hall. He ignored them. His fists balled and unclenched rhythmically.

How had she ever thought he was handsome? He was stupid. A stupid, weak, ugly toad of a man.

He rounded on her suddenly, his eyes slit malevolently. "Where's my stuff?"

She backed up a pace. In that moment, he looked capable of murder. For the first time since he'd caught her, she felt a frisson of real fear slide up her spine. "What stuff?"

He reached out and grabbed her again, giving her a shake hard enough to rattle her teeth. "You know damn well, what stuff. You're the only one who could have taken it. I don't have time to fool around. I either come up with the stuff or the money. The guy I'm dealing with won't take any more excuses."

Thoroughly frightened and confused, she stared at him. "You have something of Lenny's?"

"Lenny? I don't give a damn about Lenny." His expression was savage. "I need the bag you stole from me. Where is it? This guy plays for keeps. Now where—"

He released her so abruptly she fell backward, cutting her hand on a piece of broken crockery. She inched along the floor, cowering at his expression, but he was no longer looking at her. His eyes were fastened on something outside the house. His curse was short and frightened.

His beady gaze darted around the room as though seeking another exit. Only then did she become aware that someone was on the back porch. Abruptly, he turned and bolted for the side door.

An instinct born of survival caused her to scramble across the floor, through the dining room and into the living room. A large shadow floated past that window, as well. She couldn't prevent the sob that tore at her throat. There was someone on the front porch, too.

She scurried under the overturned couch, curling into as tight a ball as she could manage. Fear choked out everything else. The only sound she could hear was the blood pounding in her temples and her silent, internal cries for help. If she got out of this alive, she would change. She promised this with all the desperation of a dying person.

"WHAT DO YOU MEAN, we're going to steal a car? Are you out of your mind?"

Steve chuckled at Lynn's horrified expression. "If you could just see your face," he told her.

"That isn't even funny, Gregory. We're in enough trouble and you make jokes about stealing cars."

"It's no joke, but we're not going to steal it—exactly. We're just going to borrow it."

His hands were relaxed on the steering wheel, though his eyes constantly scanned the beltway in front of them.

"Are you serious?"

Steve nodded without looking over as he changed lanes, heading for an off ramp. "We don't have much choice. It isn't going to take the police long to run a trace on my license plate. And, as you so sweetly pointed out, this truck is easy to spot."

"It's an eyesore," she corrected absently. "Steve, you are not going to steal a car. I absolutely forbid it."

He grinned at her prim tone. It wasn't nice to tease her, but he couldn't help himself. She was so earnest. "Yes, Mommy."

Lynn flushed, but her lips thinned in determination. "I mean it, Steve. We're in enough trouble. We'll just do what you've been wanting to do all along and go to the police."

He turned onto the Dulles access road leading to the airport. "Too late. We should have done that before the incident at the pizza parlor." He flashed her a devil's grin. "Besides, my pride's at stake."

"What on earth does pride have to do with anything?"

The smile faded instantly. "I'm a private investigator, Lynn. A detective. If I can't figure out what's going on here, I have no right to those titles."

"That's just stupid."

Steve ignored the comment. "Besides, we have to find out what happened to your sister and Kevin."

"Kevin? I couldn't care less what happened to Kevin."

"Hasn't it dawned on you yet? The two of them may be together."

Her gray eyes widened and her protest died a quick death as it reached her lips. He watched the idea take hold.

"And then again," he went on more kindly, "one disappearance may have nothing to do with the other. But any way you look at it, we need answers and we sure won't get them sitting at police headquarters. Once they get their hands on us and this baby, they won't let us anywhere near this case."

Lynn sat up straighter and peered around. She hadn't really been paying attention to where they were going, so she was shocked to discover Steve's destination. "This is the airport. Steve, what are you doing?"

He pulled up and took a ticket from the squat machine guarding the parking lot. Her fingers accepted it from him automatically.

"We're going to borrow a car, remember?"

A lump of foreboding formed in her stomach. She stared at him, only he wasn't looking at her. His concentration was directed to the aisles as he circled the long-term parking lot. Her pulse rate picked up, sending blood shooting through her veins. He was going to do it. He was actually going to steal a car.

Suddenly, he smiled and the lines of worry smoothed out on his forehead. He gunned the engine to take them down a particular row and pulled to a stop behind a silver-gray sedan. Her mouth dropped open in protest once again, but for some reason, the words wouldn't come. Steve read off the license number and nodded to himself. Then he backed up to clear the vehicle and put his truck in park. Lynn swallowed hard, finding most of her saliva had given in to fear and gone into hiding. Steve wasn't kidding. He was actually going to steal a car.

"You're crazy," she whispered. "You can't steal that car. You can't!"

Steve leaned over. Her protest was swallowed under the sensual pressure of his lips. When she felt the probe of his tongue, she parted her lips for a taste of him. It was delicious torture. She wrapped her hands around his neck to pull him closer. She was on fire, burning with a voracious craving to touch, to stroke, to hold. Desire constricted her throat.

He pulled back slowly, as if the action caused him pain. Her hands fell from his neck reluctantly. Steve regarded her from beneath half-open lids.

She trembled, running the tip of her tongue over her lips. Tasting him. Wanting more.

He followed the movement and inhaled raggedly, as affected as she was. "We're going to set fires, Jerrilynn."

"We're going to get arrested," she muttered, trying to ignore the hammering of her pulse.

"Don't worry, I know exactly what I'm doing." He opened his door and jumped from the cab.

She couldn't tear her gaze from his. "Hah. Right now, security people are scrambling into their cars en route to this very spot. Grand theft auto. Good God."

Steve chuckled. "We aren't going to get arrested. Security is too busy keeping the departing passenger lanes clear to bother with us." He leaned forward to touch her bottom lip with his finger.

The touch was electrifying. It took supreme concentration to form a coherent thought. "Easy for you to say. I'm just a junior executive for a large accounting firm. I'm not a detective. I don't want to be one."

His beard twitched with humor. "So?"

"So junior executives have nice simple, sometimes boring, jobs. They don't run around with kidnapped babies, stealing cars—or borrowing them illegally, either."

"Or neck in the airport parking lot?" he added with a grin.

"Never."

Steve winked. "Trust me," he said, then shut the door on his laughter and strode over to the sedan with an easy, loose-limbed stride.

She watched him probe the underside of the wheel well for a minute before he produced a magnetic holder. As though it were an everyday occurrence, he unlocked the sedan and backed it out of the parking space. Then he put the truck in its place.

"Come on, we'll transfer all the stuff to the back seat." And he hefted out the case of baby formula and carried it over to the Plymouth.

Lynn didn't move. She wasn't certain that she could. His kisses had left her weak, but his actions left her shaken in a different way. He really meant to do this. He was going to steal a car. Steve returned to the truck and came around to her side of the cab to help her down. His knuckle stroked the skin of her cheek, sending a whole new set of nerves skittering.

"It's okay, Jerrilynn. We aren't really stealing. Tim's brother, Jeff, owns this car. He and his wife are on their honeymoon right now."

Steve climbed in back and began to unstrap the baby. "We're just going to borrow his car and leave my truck in its place. They're due back the day after tomorrow, so it'll be okay. Jeff knows my truck and I left him a note. Trust me."

Trust him? As if she had a choice. Lynn scooted into the car's passenger seat, trying not to touch anything.

"Don't worry," Steve said as he finished belting the car seat into place and slid in behind the wheel. "Jeff will thank us for taking the car. After all, I'm paying his enormous parking fee."

"Why doesn't that make me feel any better?"

"Look at the bright side. You didn't like riding around in my truck, anyhow. You have to admit, this is more along the lines of what you're used to. It's even the same color as your car. Besides, now we have another car with a telephone."

"Oh, joy. I can't tell you how happy that makes me."

Steve merely chuckled again. When had she lost control of her life? she wondered. "You couldn't just use a telephone booth like everyone else?"

"Cheer up. Consider this an adventure to tell your kids about one day. Things will work out. You'll see." He started the engine and lifted the built-in phone.

And promptly cursed.

"They'll work out, huh?" She shook her head, tossing back the strand of hair that was tickling one eye. "What's wrong now?"

"He put a block on it." Steve sounded offended.

A smile stole across her lips and Lynn looked down at the dead instrument in his large hand. "Does that mean what I think it does?"

Steve glowered at her. "You don't have to look so pleased. We can't use Jeff's telephone without knowing the code to disconnect the block."

Lynn settled back in her seat, still smiling. "Let me guess. It wasn't conveniently written down in the case with the key."

He set down the black receiver with an audible click. "You can be a real pain, you know that?"

"Why, thank you."

He gave her a quick glower and reached for his wallet to pay the toll. It wasn't until they were back on the beltway that either of them spoke again. "Steve, what are we going to do now?"

He took his eyes from the road for just a second. "Well, the first thing we need is that bolt hole."

"What?"

His beard twitched and she suspected he was trying not to laugh. "A place to hide," he explained.

"Oh." She mulled that over for a second. "We could go to my parents' house. They won't be back until the beginning of next month."

Steve debated. The police might or might not take the time to check out Lynn's relatives. But even if they did, they certainly wouldn't stake them out.

"It might be safe. It's worth taking a look at. Give me some directions."

Her parents lived in Chevy Chase in an older, established neighborhood where graceful old cherry trees lined the street, their twisted branches spanning the road to form a dense canopy overhead. Buds were already on the branches due to the unusual heat of the early-spring weather.

"I'll bet this street is something to see when these trees bloom," Steve commented.

"It's like a fairyland," Lynn agreed. "My parents are often trapped in the house by all the tourists who drive past."

The Rothmore family home was near the far end of the block. A maroon Ford sedan rested in the driveway. Lynn straightened to attention.

"Steve, that's Marcy's car!" Her excitement was infectious.

"Good. Now maybe we can get some answers." Steve pulled up behind the Ford and killed the engine. Instinct, habit, maybe it was plain old caution, but something, made him pause. As Lynn started toward the house, he laid a restraining hand on her arm.

"What are you doing?"

Steve surveyed the brick structure and the surrounding area. Huge boxwoods outlined the front of the house, forming an impenetrable hedge. There were large rhododendrons running the length of one side of the building and a large, ornamental Japanese maple tree hugged the ground on the other side. It was a burglar's paradise, with all this heavy old shrubbery. There were plenty of places to hide.

"Steve?"

He couldn't explain the sense of wrongness emanating from the setting. He only knew he didn't want to walk blithely up those steps, onto that small porch and into that house without taking some precautions.

"Here. Take Rachel." He handed her the car seat. "Let me scout it out a bit first."

"What are you talking about? This is my parents' house. Marcy's inside."

He shook his head and captured her eyes with his own. "Maybe. I just have a bad feeling about this, Lynn. Remember the apartments? I want you to wait here for a few minutes, okay?"

No sprang to mind, but Lynn found the word stuck in her throat. Steve's forehead was creased with concern, and his lips formed a stiff, thin line. The panther was back, she thought, and on the prowl. There was a coiled expectancy about him as he studied the house where she had grown up. She shifted the car seat to her other hand and stopped moving.

"Thanks." Steve gave her shoulder a quick caress. "Wait here. I'll be right back."

His eyes scrutinized the bushes and surroundings, watching for any sign of movement. Everything was still and expectant, even the air. Nothing moved behind any of the windows, either, yet the sense of danger slid along his nerve endings, making the fingers of his left hand itch with the need to close over his gun.

He mounted the three steps to the small porch in a single fluid movement. Instead of going directly to the door, he flattened himself along the wall and peered through the nearest window. The sheer drapes made it difficult to see inside, but not impossible.

The destruction was familiar. He'd already seen the same sight twice today, only this time the perpetrator hadn't gone in through the front door. There was no sign of tampering around the dead bolt.

Probably a window, he decided. And because of Marcy's car sitting in the driveway, he didn't think he'd find the house empty the way he had found the two apartments. He had a feeling that the house was dangerously occupied, and he didn't consider Marcy the danger.

Carefully, he tried the doorknob. He hadn't expected it to turn and it didn't. On silent feet, he crossed to the far side of the porch and swung lithely over the edge and down. He didn't remember reaching for it, but his gun was now comfortably in his hand as he skirted the side of the house, heading toward the back. He scrutinized the windows for signs of broken glass, figuring the person inside would have picked an inconspicuous window through which to enter.

And then again, the side door opened with no resistance when he tried the knob. There was absolute silence from within, but Steve didn't holster his gun. He mounted the short flight of steps that led to the kitchen, hoping he'd guessed right and shouldn't have gone down to check out the basement first.

Someone very angry had torn through the house. The kitchen was a disaster. Steve picked his way carefully through the debris. In the dining room, he came face-to-face with an enlarged family portrait prominently displayed on one wall. The two sisters did look enough alike to be twins—until you looked closely.

Marcy had a weak face, he decided. Lynn was much prettier.

This was obviously a lived-in family home. The wanton destruction made him furious. He paused in the hall between the living room and dining room to listen again. There was no sound of anyone moving about. A glance around the living room showed that the vandal had been content to knock over furniture and pull knickknacks off the shelves of a handsome wall unit.

The sense that he wasn't alone in the house was still strong. He paused to listen before ascending the staircase. There was no sound from overhead.

The destruction hadn't reached all the rooms. The first bedroom had been converted into a sewing room and everything was in its proper place. The second bedroom looked like a guest room. It, too, was untouched. The third room had been decimated. It still bore the frilly touches that marked it as a young woman's room—in ruins now.

If he had to make a guess, based on the makeup and clothing strewn everywhere, he'd say this was Marcy's old room. He probed around for a minute, but found nothing useful. In the master bedroom, the vandal apparently had been interrupted before he'd barely started. Had that someone found what they were looking for? Or had he stopped because of Marcy's arrival—or Steve's own? Could Marcy be the one tearing things up?

He liked this less and less, but at least he hadn't fallen over any bodies. Steve realized that subconsciously he'd been braced for that very thing. His sense of unease, however, was still very strong as he started back down the stairs. He hoped Lynn had had the sense to stay put.

Then he heard the gunshots.

LYNN FOLLOWED Steve's movements anxiously from beside Marcy's car. When the gun appeared in his hand, she wanted to cry out. Only her faith in him, and the presence of the tiny baby, held her still and silent. She did trust Steve. If Marcy was inside, he'd do what he could to protect her sister. Only, what had he seen when he'd peered in the window?

Lynn's tension escalated as he went around the side of the house. He tried the side door, which swung open easily at his touch, and disappeared from view. She barely breathed, waiting for him to reappear.

"Come on, Steve."

Long minutes passed. The baby began to fret in the direct sunlight. Still, Steve didn't come out.

"I know just how you feel," she told Rachel as she moved to the far side of Marcy's car. She set the car seat under a nearby tree. At least it offered some shade. "I want him to come back outside, too. Come on, Steve. Get out here. Give me a sign. What's going on?"

Suddenly, a running man burst from the protective cover of the heavy bushes on the far side of the house. He flew across the lawn, casting a quick, furtive look in the direction from which he'd appeared.

"Kevin!"

Shock blunted his broad, flat face, normally set in phony, earnest lines. Then his expression twisted. Fear and anger, almost hatred, covered his face.

He yanked her arm before she realized what he intended. "Get in the car! Get in the car!" He wrenched open the car door with one hand and began to drag her forward.

"No!"

He spun her around with shocking strength, and forced her inside. Fear for the baby minimized her resistance. She scampered across the seat, intending to jump out the other side, but Kevin's frightened oath made her pause. She followed his frozen stare to the figure that came chasing out from behind the hedge at the far corner of the house. The pursuer was small and wiry and was wearing a green windbreaker. Lynn saw nothing beyond that as the man brought up the barrel of a large gun to aim in their direction.

Lynn ducked. Kevin twisted the key and threw the car into gear with a lurch. She heard the sound of shots even as the car screeched in reverse down the driveway. The man fired again then raced across the grass, heading for a red sporty-looking car parked in front of the house next door. That was the last she saw as Kevin floored Jeff's silver car and tore off down the narrow street.

STEVE TOOK the final steps in a single jump. One foot landed on a baking sheet and he slid, out of control, across the brightly waxed floor. The gun fell from his fingers and clattered across the tile. He used both hands to grab for the banister and managed to stop his slide and certain fall, but nearly yanked his shoulder apart in the effort. He stood perfectly still for a second, in shock, grateful that the safety was still on so the gun hadn't discharged and shot him in the leg.

Moving stiffly, Steve grabbed the weapon and fumbled at the front-door lock. He spotted Jeff's car pulling out of the driveway at a high rate of speed. A small red Camaro launched itself in pursuit.

Heart pounding, Steve raced toward the driveway, hoping in vain that Lynn would be standing someplace unharmed. She wasn't. No one was. In this sleepy, quiet neighborhood, nothing stirred. Even the gunshots hadn't caused a commotion.

With an oath, he turned back to Marcy's car, and Rachel began to cry. With shaky, thankful hands, he lifted the car seat. Rachel's tiny face was screwed tight in anger, but she was unhurt.

"Lynn!"

There was no answer to his call. She would never abandon the baby—not if she could help it. And he was the one who had left Jeff's key in the ignition.

No keys handily dangled from the ignition of Marcy's car, but at least it was unlocked. His right shoulder protested as he strapped the baby in the front seat. He was uncomfortably aware of his strained muscles, even as his fingers fumbled under the dash for the necessary wires. He hadn't hot-wired a car since a buddy had shown him how to do it when he was in the air force.

Where were those damn wires?

His fingers found what he was looking for. It was probably too late to catch them, but he had to try. And he couldn't help thinking that this was the third car he'd be driving in as many hours. It had to be some kind of record.

A SCREAM FORCED its way past Lynn's shocked lips as they careened around the corner and into the path of an oncoming delivery truck. Luck, rather than skill, kept them from becoming pinned under its large wheels.

"Kevin! Stop! You're going to kill us!"

"Shut up! Just shut up!" he screamed. His lips pulled savagely away from his teeth as he fought to maintain control of the car at a dangerously high speed. Lynn started to heave a sigh as they approached the main intersection. Could she leap from the car?

It didn't matter. Kevin not only didn't stop, he didn't even slow down. He zipped out onto the main thoroughfare with no regard for stop signs or oncoming traffic.

This time, she didn't try to blunt the scream. "Oh, my God, slow down!"

"Shut up," Kevin snarled. He weaved in and out of traffic so dangerously that even a moment's distraction would send them into another vehicle for sure. Lynn shut up.

As they sped through a red light to the blare of oncoming horns, Lynn managed to contain her next scream so it echoed only inside her head. She hunkered down as terror clogged her throat. She prayed Steve was safe. She prayed he had found Rachel unharmed. She prayed that she would survive the collision she was certain would happen at any moment. There was nothing she could do to stop the maniac behind the wheel of Jeff's car.

LADY LUCK SAT on his shoulders as Steve strained to catch up. He tried to swallow his fear when he spotted

Jeff's car at an intersection more than a mile up the road. It darted into the path of oncoming traffic. In his head he heard the scream of brakes and the strident sound of horns. The driver of the silver car seemed oblivious to the danger. The silver car made it. The small red car riding its bumper wasn't as lucky. Steve cringed.

A heavy brown sedan swerved desperately, leaving a burgundy station wagon nowhere to go. Steve stood on his own brakes when, with a shriek of grinding metal, the three cars in the intersection collided and spun out of control. Glass and metal debris spewed across the asphalt, leaving the street up ahead blocked.

With a curse, he gave the empty street behind him a quick glance before he reversed direction. There was another side street he had just passed and with any luck, he could take it over a block and avoid the collision. Traffic wouldn't be getting around that mess in any hurry and the need to catch Lynn was like a living force inside him, but he couldn't risk a crash with the baby in the car.

"Hang on, Rachel." Her cries had died to soft baby whimpers.

Fate smiled on him in a moment of whimsy. The side street he had chosen not only intersected with the main road, but it came out at a traffic light just beyond the accident scene. Fate even went so far as to turn the light green as he sped toward it.

As he made it through the intersection, he spotted the silver car a long way in front of them. Their speed in the heavy traffic took his breath away.

"Damn it, you're safe," he muttered. "The sedan and the station wagon took him out of the action. Slow down. Geez!"

Steve swallowed hard as the other car plunged through a red light and barely avoided colliding head-on with a pickup truck.

"Lynn, for crying out loud. Slow down!"

Who the hell was driving that car? Lynn? Marcy? If it was Lynn, he'd blister her hide. She was bleaching his hair with her antics.

Only, he didn't think it was Lynn behind the wheel. She might hide a fiery nature beneath her sophisticated veneer, but he doubted she also hid the ability or the inclination to be a LeMans driver. Of course, being shot at can motivate a person.

The vehicle weaved in and out of traffic and paid no mind to traffic lights. Unfortunately, Steve didn't have that choice. Trapped behind a string of cars, he could only watch helplessly as Jeff's small sedan barreled away.

He saw the car round a corner and disappear. He closed his eyes in frustration. When he tasted blood, he realized he must have bitten his lip. His fingers clamped around the steering wheel as though permanently affixed, and his body practically vibrated with tension.

Where were they going? He would lose them now in this traffic—if they didn't crash first. The light changed, but no one else on the road seemed to be in any hurry. He fumed uselessly. Only Rachel's presence kept him from attempting to pass illegally. The driver of Jeff's car might slow down if he didn't see further pursuit.

Who was driving that car?

Hell, it could be anyone. A more important question was, who had been shooting guns? Lynn must be terrified. If she was hurt...

Steve turned the corner where Jeff's car had vanished. His open hand smacked the steering wheel as he studied the traffic situation in front of him. Four blocks down, everything had ground to a halt. There was no sign of the silver sedan, but there were definite signs of its passage. A small Ford truck lay on its side in the middle of the street. It had apparently collided with a Toyota, whose driver had then taken out a green Voyager. He couldn't tell if the blue cab was also involved or had just stopped short of the pileup.

"Lynn."

There wasn't a doubt in his mind as to the cause of the accident, but Jeff's car was long gone. Traffic was completely stalled ahead of him, but there was a gas station to his right. Steve drove through the gas station and out onto the side exit.

He had no idea where this road led, but hopefully, it would run into another one that would put him back on the main drag beyond the accident scene. It had worked before.

Where the devil was Lynn headed?

Come to that, where was he going? The road was circuitous. Every twist caused the knot in his stomach to tighten a little further. His tension was almost at the snapping point, when he found his way back onto Wisconsin Avenue. Of course, there was no sign of Lynn or of Jeff's small vehicle.

An overwhelming sense of impending disaster caused him to continue skimming down the street, scanning parking lots and side streets for a glimpse of the silvery car. He had to find her.

"Come on, Lynn. Come on, honey. Show me where you are. Please, sweetheart. Leave me a sign."

Lady Luck was in a fickle mood. The streets were dotted with silvery sedans, but none of them was the right vehicle. Lynn had simply vanished.

Chapter Six

The house had been silent a long time now. Cautiously, she wriggled out from under the couch, shivering with fear. A tear of self-pity drifted down the familiar track. He'd be back. She knew that. And this time, she might not get away so easily. He was crazy. She rubbed her arms where he'd left bruises. Well, she wouldn't give him another chance. She'd get away. This time, she'd hide someplace safe. Someplace where no one could find her.

It took a bit of searching, but eventually, she found her mother's extra credit card. She was angry there was so little cash to go with it.

"Why is this happening to me?"

The walls refused to answer as she stuffed a few items of clothing into a spare suitcase. Her hand, where she'd cut it, stung with every movement, sending fresh tears coursing down her face. It wasn't fair. She needed another pill to calm her down—to help her think and plan.

Outside, she came to a quivering halt. Someone had taken her car! She stamped her foot in fury before her eyes riveted on the small blue car two doors down. He took her car and left his? Why? Well, she still had a set of his keys upstairs in her old bedroom.

Angrily, she cursed as she drove with reckless abandon. At a traffic light several blocks away, her fingers groped on the opposite seat. They encountered only the nubby material of the seat. Her head pivoted in surprise. Ignoring the changing light and the blare of car horns behind her, she bent down, searching the floor for the fallen bag. And then she remembered. This was his car, not hers. The bag was in her car. That was why he had taken it. Panic threatened to choke off her breathing. What was she going to do?

LYNN STUDIED Kevin from under lowered lashes and felt a renewed flash of fear. This was no longer her sister's ingratiating boyfriend. This Kevin was a frightening stranger. The stream of vitriolic words that issued from his lips left her cold and shaken. She had no idea what he was droning on about, only that Marcy had something that belonged to him and he was going to kill her when he got his hands on her again.

Well, she had to admit, that did seem to be the prevailing attitude, where Marcy was concerned. And, at any other time, she would ignore his words as so much hot air. Just now, however, she thought Kevin looked perfectly capable of murder. Kevin had changed from a sneaky jerk to a serious potential danger.

"That should do it," he announced, looking into the rearview mirror with a self-satisfied nod. Lynn didn't know what he meant and she didn't care. She was just grateful that he'd stopped driving as though he were auditioning for the part of someone's stunt double.

"He won't catch us now," Kevin stated. He took his eyes from the road to study his passenger. "The question is, what am I going to do with you, huh, big sister?'' His momentary appraisal made her flesh crawl.

''You never liked me, did you?'' he asked scornfully. ''Well, let me tell you something, the feeling's been mutual. You're just a snotty little bitch who needs taking down a peg or two.''

He turned his attention back to the road in time to avoid a collision with a UPS truck. He swore viciously at the blameless driver before turning back to her. His hand snaked out to grab her arm in a fierce grip. Lynn recoiled from his touch as far as she was able and he grinned—an evil grin meant to scare her.

''You're going to pay.''

His words cut like a knife, but she refused to show any fear. ''Well, you're going to jail.''

The vein at his temple twitched ominously as he took the next corner too fast. He let go of her arm and Lynn debated whether or not to wrench open the door and fling herself from the car. His words stopped her.

''Where'd you get the kid?'' he growled.

She didn't think he had even noticed the baby when he grabbed her. So why hadn't he grabbed Rachel, as well?

''As if you didn't know.''

He looked genuinely puzzled, a look that quickly changed to a frown of contemplation. ''It doesn't matter. I'll have to get rid of you,'' he muttered. The cold statement heightened her fear.

Kevin steered the car into the parking lot of a seedy motel. Lynn was ready. The moment he braked and thrust the car into park, she was on him, nails going for his eyes.

She missed, but he hollered as she tore a strip down his face. Her other hand grabbed for the ignition key.

His blow sent her backward against the window on the passenger side.

"You bitch!"

He reached for her as her hand yanked the door handle. She tumbled from the car. He came across the seat after her, blood running from the scratches on his face. His features were murderous.

She stumbled, trying to get to her feet, when her hand landed on a loose stone. Her fingers closed over it as he lunged after her and she threw it. The blow caught him in the temple. With a bellow of rage, he jumped back. Lynn was up and running. She had to find help.

Kevin came after her. Surely someone would notice. She had no breath left to scream. She rushed toward Wisconsin Avenue. Oh, God, there were no pedestrians. Kevin's hands grabbed her from behind as she reached the sidewalk. He spun her around and his open-hand slap connected in a stinging blow with her left cheek. Off-balance, she would have tumbled to the ground if he hadn't gripped her arm.

She pummeled him with her fists, the key extended between her fingers, trying again for his eyes. He dragged her across the parking lot to the room, where he fumbled for his room key. She kicked at his shin with all the force she could muster. At the same time, she twisted sideways, trying to break his steely grip.

For such a lean man, Kevin was unexpectedly strong. Instead of breaking free, she only succeeded in further enraging him. He slammed her back against the doorframe. His hand came up to slap her face once more. The door opened at her back and Lynn toppled inside. She landed on the threadbare carpet.

Kevin bent over her in a crazed fury. She struck out at his face, the key clenched between her fingers like a weapon. He twisted to the side and she saw a second form fill the doorway behind him. Kevin was yanked backward so hard he careened into the window with enough force to crack the glass.

Lynn scrambled to her feet and flattened herself against the wall. A Steve she barely recognized reached for Kevin again. The panther was out for blood. He yanked Kevin forward into the force of the fist aimed for the smaller man's stomach. Kevin doubled over with a grunt, falling headfirst into Steve. They tumbled onto the bed.

Lynn wanted to turn away, but helpless fascination made her watch as Steve lit into Kevin with a fury that shook the walls.

"Whadaya think you're doing there, mister? I sent Jenny to call the cops."

The interruption was enough for Kevin to land a solid blow to Steve's face. In the doorway, holding a rag and a can of spray cleaner, stood a large woman in sloppy jeans and a baggy man's shirt.

With blood streaming from his nose as well as his cheek, Kevin shoved Steve backward and tore past Lynn, knocking the cleaning woman to the ground.

Steve cursed and started after him, but stopped when he saw Lynn. His chest heaved. There was a tear along the seam of his sweatshirt. A bruise was already starting to swell next to his left eye, and his disheveled hair stuck up at weird angles. He looked uncompromisingly large and male, and more menacing than she had ever seen him.

"Are you okay?"

She gave a jerky nod. He shut his eyes and pulled her close in a quick embrace. Nothing had ever felt so good, so safe. Lynn felt his lips on her hair, then he pulled away to look at her. There was a ferocity to his expression that startled her as he quickly released her. He was moving toward the door before she could decide what it meant. He stepped outside and helped the flustered woman to her feet. "Are you hurt?"

The cleaning woman shook her head, both chins quivering. At the other end of the stretch of units, Steve saw a portly man start out of the main office. He turned to Lynn. "Come on, sweetheart, we need to get to the police station. This time, your ex-husband has gone too far. I'm pressing charges."

Lynn gaped at him. So did the woman. Steve took Lynn's elbow and propelled her over to Jeff's silver car. To the woman, he added, "When the police come, please be sure to press your own charges against him for assault and any damages."

The manager shouted. The baby wailed from the front seat of Marcy's car. The police would show up at any moment.

"You'll need this." Lynn thrust the key into his hand. His expression went from surprise to a broad grin of appreciation.

"You're incredible." He gave her a quick hug before he thrust her inside and ran for the baby. He was straightening up with the carrier, when a white drugstore bag caught his eye. It had fallen to the floor, and a gold chain spilled from the opening. He snatched the bag and ran for Jeff's car.

"At least I won't have to hot-wire this car, too, thanks to you."

The manager had almost reached them. Steve could see his glasses bouncing against the bridge of his nose as he drew closer. Steve threw the car into gear and took off. There was no sign of Kevin.

Steve winced as he bumped his hand against the steering wheel. A quick look showed his knuckles were bruised and slightly swollen, probably from connecting with Kevin's nose. He sincerely hoped he'd broken it.

Lynn hung over the back seat trying to soothe the enraged child. A glance in her direction told him that soon the baby wouldn't be the only one crying.

He cupped Lynn's shoulder gently and she jumped before she swung to face him. Those wide gray eyes had a bruised quality to them. The lovely long lashes were damp with moisture.

Steve cursed and she flinched.

"I'll kill him."

"No." Frantically, she protested his cold statement. "I'm fine. Really." She brushed at her eyes, trying to still the fine tremor of her fingers.

"You're a lot better than fine, Lynn. You're one hell of a woman."

"In this case, I'd rather have been a hell of a boxer."

Her smile was lopsided and endearing. He reached out, took her hand, and only then saw the blood from her broken fingernails.

"You're hurt!"

She followed his glance. "Not as bad as I will be when my manicurist sees this mess."

The quaver in her voice belied her brave words. "I need to see to Rachel."

Reluctantly, Steve let her hand go as she turned around again. Steve tugged at his beard, dimly aware that his shoulder hurt like the devil and he could actually feel the skin swelling next to his eye where Kevin had landed his one solid punch. Great. They both looked as if they'd been in a fight. So much for keeping a low profile.

He studied the neighborhood, recognized where they were and spotted a Holiday Inn ahead. Quickly, he maneuvered the car into the large, busy lot.

"What are you doing?" Lynn asked.

Steve swallowed his churning rage at Kevin. The need to comfort Lynn was more powerful. He drew her chin gently back to face him. "Come here." She went into his arms with a deep shuddering breath, and he stroked the reddened area where Kevin had struck her. "You're the strongest, bravest, smartest woman I've ever known." Steve pressed a gentle kiss on her lips.

The sweet, responsive taste of her was almost his undoing. He drew back reluctantly when she would have let him deepen the kiss.

"No, ma'am," he whispered. "You're too much temptation for a parking lot. Our last kiss nearly melted my toenails."

Color mounted her throat to spread over her cheeks.

"Lynn, I want you to go inside and rent us a room."

"Why?"

"This is as good a bolt hole as any." He pulled out his wallet and fished for a credit card. "You'll have to sign us in as husband and wife."

Her eyes whipped up to meet his.

"I know what you're thinking, but you're wrong."

She cocked her head.

"This is business, Lynn."

"Business."

He nodded. "We need a bolt hole."

"A hotel room?"

"Why not? Look what happened when we went to your mother's place."

Her face paled. Gingerly, his fingers touched the puffiness on her cheek. "I'm sorry, sweetheart. But we need a place to crash. My sweatshirt's ripped and I'm sure I look as bruised as I feel."

Lynn flinched, but her eyes were drawn automatically to the hint of bare skin revealed near his collarbone and then to the darkening skin around his eye. Recalling how the damage had been done made her cringe. The images were indelibly etched in her mind.

"Besides," Steve continued, "the police are looking for a couple with a baby. If you go in there alone, you won't stand out in anyone's mind—as long as you keep your damaged fingernails from sight. If someone does notice, tell them you had to change a tire."

Lynn glared.

"Well, with this beard, and my bruised face, I'd stand out."

"Are you saying I'm unmemorable?"

Steve had the grace to look embarrassed. "I didn't mean it that way, I meant—"

"I know exactly what you meant." She opened the car door. "But you're going to pay for a suite," she warned him.

Steve raised an eyebrow, relieved at the resurgence of her spirit. "Okay by me. After all, we need someplace for the baby to sleep."

Her teeth snapped together with an audible click to prevent an answering retort. Instantly, his expression gentled. He smiled and dispensed a wink. "Trust me."

Lynn tossed him a quelling look and gazed down at the credit card in her hand. Trust him, indeed.

"You should be worried about trusting me."

His mouth opened in surprise.

"Personally, I hope they have a presidential suite," she said, starting to close the door.

"Lynn," he said seriously. "Don't mention the baby. Just check us in as a husband and wife."

She nodded and took a moment to straighten her clothing. Hopefully, she would look as though she had just hit town after a long drive.

The young girl was most obliging when Lynn asked for a suite. It helped that the girl was the only one at the desk and the phone kept her hopping. She never asked a single personal question. They were assigned a suite on the fifth floor of the seven-story building. As luck would have it, the elevator they needed to take wasn't anywhere near the reception desk.

"I don't think I'll ask what this is going to cost," Steve said, looking around.

To Lynn, it didn't seem particularly fancy. Other than the addition of a spacious sitting room, it still resembled the impersonal interiors of nearly every hotel she had ever stayed in.

"I tried to get a room on the first floor, but this was the lowest level they had available. I told them my husband had trouble with elevators because he's claustrophobic and stairs were out of the question because his artificial leg doesn't fit properly."

Steve stopped moving and turned to gape at her. "You didn't."

Lynn smiled sweetly and turned her attention to the baby.

"You're kidding, right?"

The baby continued to fuss. Lynn ignored him.

"Lynn, tell me you're kidding."

"I didn't mention the baby, but if she keeps crying like this, they're going to know we have one."

Steve muttered something under his breath. "Don't worry. We won't disturb anyone right now. The businesspeople are in meetings and the tourists are out sightseeing at this hour. Tell me you were joking."

Lynn didn't crack a smile. She felt brittle, stretched to the end of her tolerance. And the baby kept crying. She shifted Rachel from one arm to the other. How Steve thought they were going to get away with staying here and have no one notice they had a baby, she couldn't fathom.

"Come on, Rachel, be a good girl. I don't know what you want." The crying was beginning to shred her frazzled nerves. She felt exhausted. If Rachel didn't stop crying soon, Lynn was going to sit on the overstuffed chair and give in to a fit of the bawls herself. She paced, jiggling the baby, who continued to yell. Steve set down the box of formula and the other baby paraphernalia he'd unloaded from the car. Lynn spun on him in frustration.

"She doesn't need changing, she doesn't want more food, what's the matter with her?"

"She's just exercising her lungs," he said softly. "After all, she's been jostled around a lot lately, and she wants us to know she's annoyed."

Exasperated, Lynn set the baby back in her car seat on the nubby couch and strode across the room to stand in front of him. "Just how would you know that?"

"I was a baby once myself."

"That isn't funny."

Steve noted the lines of strain around Lynn's mouth and eyes. Up to now, she'd handled each situation like a trouper, but it was obvious Lynn had had enough.

"Come here," he told her quietly, all teasing gone. She didn't move. She looked so vulnerable it tore at his heart. His smile felt crooked as he ran a knuckle down her smooth cheek. "It's okay, Lynn. It's been a long day for all of us."

Her tears were near the surface. Her lovely long lashes were damp with unshed moisture. "The baby—"

"Will be fine." He looked over at Rachel and saw she had fallen asleep.

"Oh, God." A single glittery tear tracked its way down Lynn's cheek.

He cradled her against his chest, stroking her slender back. She shuddered and he rested his chin on her bowed head. He could love this woman, he realized. "It's okay, Lynn. Really. Everything's going to work out."

She drew back and lifted tired eyes to his.

"Why don't you lie down in the bedroom for a few minutes while the baby is sleeping?" he suggested. "You've had a rough day."

"I'm fine, Steve."

He smiled at the tilt of her chin, the determination so plainly visible in her expressive eyes. "That you are."

Did she lift her lips or did his descend? Lynn didn't care as they met in a kiss of tender reassurance. She shivered. He smelled so good, felt so strong. She trailed her hands across the broad plane of his back, pulling him closer.

Gently, he withdrew. His voice was whiskey soft. "God, but you're a powerful temptation."

Lynn blinked, a shaky finger pressed instinctively to lips that tingled. How could she tell him that she found him devastating? That every time he kissed her, she wanted more. "Your beard tickles." She stroked the soft bristles, and his lips parted in an easy smile that warmed her heart.

He rubbed a finger across her chin. "It's leaving marks, too."

"I don't mind." She didn't. She was focused on the spreading emotions clutching her heart.

His eyes darkened. Just then, Rachel made a sound, startling both of them. Regretfully, Steve released Lynn and stepped back to look at the baby. She was still asleep, her lips curved upward.

"I told you she'd be all right."

"So you did."

"Tell me something. How did Kevin get in the car this afternoon?"

She felt a flash of regret for the lost moment, but she explained what had happened. His jaw clenched and his fists balled at his sides, reminding her how effectively he could use those fists against an enemy.

"I'm sorry, Lynn."

"It wasn't your fault."

"Yeah. It was. I knew something was wrong when we pulled up. I felt it. I should have gotten you and Rachel out of there before going inside."

She jutted her chin and placed her hands on her hips to glare at him. "Protect the little woman at all costs, huh? Did it ever occur to you that I wouldn't have let you?"

Ruefully, he looked at her. "Sorry again," he said mildly. "I was raised on tales of King Arthur's court. My mother was a romantic. Chivalry, and all that. Anyhow, we should be safe enough here for a while, and you might want to get some rest while you can."

"What are you going to do?"

"I," he announced, "am going out to make a quick phone call to try and let my boss know what's going on."

Her stomach knotted.

"We're safe here, Lynn. I promise."

"Then why don't you just call him from the phone in the bedroom?" She pointed to the nightstand and the beige telephone that hunkered between a clock and a tall lamp.

"Because I don't want anything I do traced back to O'Hearity Investigations. If I'm going to get in trouble, I don't want them drawn in, too."

"Oh."

"Don't worry. I'm just cautious by nature. Get some rest. I won't be gone long."

Lynn looked into the well of his eyes, and nodded slowly.

"What about the baby?"

They regarded the sleeping infant. "I'll lay her on the couch and pull this chair over on the off chance she can roll over. That way, she won't fall off the couch. She'll be okay there for a while."

"You'll hurry back?"

"Promise." His kiss was whisper soft. Then he picked up the key and closed the door as he left the room.

Steve didn't have to drive far before finding a gas station. Jeff's car was below a quarter of a tank, and after recent events, Steve didn't want to be caught short. The pay phone was off to one side.

"O'Hearity Investigations."

"Theresa, this is Steve Gregory. Don't you dare hang up on me."

"Oh, Mr. Gregory. I am so sorry. I really am. I just tried to—"

"Theresa, I don't care about that. Where is Tim?"

"Tim?"

"Mr. O'Hearity. Your boss?"

"Yes, sir. I mean, I know, sir. I'm sorry, sir."

Steve pulled on his beard hard enough to hurt himself. "Theresa!" It came out a bark. There was a gasp of air on the other end and then silence. Steve called on every ounce of patience he had. "Theresa," he said more kindly, "just tell me where the boss is."

"I don't know..." The words trailed off into a sniffle.

Very deliberately, Steve relaxed his death grip on the telephone. With as much gentleness as he could muster, he asked, "Did he say when he was coming back?"

"No, sir." Her voice was thick with—hopefully—unshed tears. Steve felt like a brute.

"Okay. Thanks, Theresa. Don't worry about it. I'll call him later."

He hung up and watched a pretty red-haired woman filling her car with gas. The tight blue knit dress fit her like a cashmere glove. A very happy glove at that. She was tall and leggy, and she tossed her heavy mane of hair with a casual hand as she returned his look assessingly. He didn't notice when the look turned inviting. In his mind he was seeing a different woman altogether. A woman with soft brown hair and a lush figure that she hid beneath tailored suits and mannish clothing. A woman that had invaded every facet of his being.

To think he'd lusted after redheads all these years.

Deliberately, he put Lynn out of his mind. There was a strip shopping center only a few blocks away. It seemed prudent to lay in a few things they might need.

Buying women's lingerie was not a good way of putting Lynn from his thoughts, he discovered. It took real willpower to stop at the basics. There was a peach teddy that made him think about the sexy black one he had seen hanging from her shower rod. He really wanted to see Lynn in that teddy. And he hadn't forgotten about the black dress. He fingered a silky blue robe. Damn. He really needed to get out of this department.

He did better in the men's section, but found himself hesitating again in the baby department. Rachel would look adorable in some of those tiny outfits.

Traffic had picked up tremendously by the time he left the shopping center. Rush hour, even outside the beltway, was no joke. While he sat at a particularly long light, he noticed the bag from Marcy's car.

He lifted it from the floor where it had wedged against the seat and peered inside.

Instantly, he heard Lynn telling him she believed Kevin had stolen her sapphire earrings and necklace. Steve stared hard at the small blue sapphires winking up at him in the waning sunlight and had to force his jaw muscles to relax. He didn't know who the other pieces belonged to, but he'd take bets none of them was Marcy's. The ruby-and-diamond pendant looked expensive, and certainly not something a young woman would select. The gold necklace was probably Lynn's, but he couldn't see her wearing the other two pieces.

Apparently, Lynn didn't know her sister as well as she liked to think. Steve reached back inside the bag and pulled out two large pill vials and two large economy-size ibuprofen bottles. This time, he didn't try to keep his jaw from clenching. Ignoring the exhaust fumes swirling around him, he read the labels and opened the first vial.

Kevin Goldlund might have needed penicillin tablets at one time as the prescription label indicated, but what Steve was holding cupped in his hand was something else altogether. He wasn't an authority, but he recognized amphetamines when he saw them. Uppers. Street pills. Something to make an addict feel better.

"Damn."

Both bottles of ibuprofen contained the same thing.

It could have been worse, he supposed, but it was bad enough. Taken frequently, these drugs were every bit as addictive as cocaine, and produced a similar effect. In this quantity, the pills probably had a street value of a couple thousand dollars. They were large bottles, and all four were almost completely full.

Who did they belong to, Kevin, or Marcy? Or maybe neither. In this quantity, combined with the stolen jewelry, it pointed to either someone with a serious habit, or someone with a budding career as a drug pusher and thief.

He poured the pills back inside and twisted the lids into place. Tension churned his stomach as he closed the distance between his car and the one in front of it. His fingers drummed a useless tattoo against the steering wheel. All of a sudden, he had a strong need to get back to Lynn and Rachel.

Impatient, he scanned the sidewalks as a new thought intruded. He was only a few blocks away from the Holiday Inn, which was only a few blocks from the motel where Kevin had taken Lynn.

Was it possible Kevin had seen Lynn register? Worse, had he seen Steve leave?

The image of this morning's scene sent cold fury mixed with genuine fear coursing through him.

"I told her she'd be safe."

His hand clenched over the steering wheel. If Kevin hurt her again, he'd kill the man with his bare hands.

Chapter Seven

The wound in his side was making him miserable. He rose and turned on the telly. He hadn't seen a news report for several days now, but he was in time to catch most of the five-o'clock broadcast. What he heard caused his head to swivel, his soft drink forgotten halfway to his mouth.

"Bloody damn it to hell. Who the bleeding hell is Jerrilynn Rothmore?"

He had only caught a glimpse of the picture they flashed on-screen, but the woman the police were looking for was a dead ringer for the girl who fled the house with the baby. He swore at the room in general and drained his glass, wishing it was something other than soda. The bright red handbag sat in plain sight on the table. He snapped open the wallet and withdrew the driver's license. Marcellina Rothmore, not Jerrilynn. He fished inside for her address book. There was no Jerrilynn listed. There was, however, a Lynn. He sank back down on the chair.

Were they one and the same? The red-haired man cursed roundly and pounded his fist on the table, knocking over the empty can of cola and causing the glass to bounce, sloshing soda on the tabletop. How much more could go wrong? Who else was involved? Was it too late to salvage the situation?

He uttered another curse. Had Lenny been following Marcellina or Jerrilynn? Stupid question. Lenny had been following the baby, not the woman. But if Jerrilynn had Rachel, what had happened to Marcellina? And who was the bearded man? What the bloody devil was going on here?

He stood and began to pace. His side throbbed and pulled with a pain he was coming to expect. He knotted one hand into a fist and pounded it into his other open palm.

What should he do now? What could he do now? He wanted to hit something a lot more satisfying than his own palm. Fear and uncertainty twisted his insides like a living, writhing creature. The thought of an American prison terrified him. He was fairly certain Lenny wouldn't talk, but then again...

Maybe he should take steps to be absolutely positive of that. And he must decide what to do about the baby. Going after the tyke meant chasing down Jerrilynn Rothmore. The police were already trying to do just that.

Damn. He couldn't give up. There was more than all that money at stake. He absolutely had to get the baby. But first, he needed to get rid of Lenny. The man was a liability now. He looked around the room and spotted his jacket. Lenny first. He'd get that distasteful chore out of the way and tackle Jerrilynn Rothmore next.

LYNN DRIFTED SLOWLY out of sleep, aware of a heavy weight pressing down on her waist. The spicy scent of after-shave filled her nostrils. Instinctively, her sleepy body snuggled closer to the warmth alongside her. The heavy weight of an arm tightened protectively.

She opened drowsy eyes to face equally misty ones peering at her from under thick lashes. "You smell good," she told him softly.

His smile was heartbreakingly sweet. His hand moved to cup the back of her head as he pulled her firmly toward him.

"So do you," he whispered, his voice thick with languid passion.

And his voice brought her all the way up from the haven of sleep to find her fingers tracing a path down his firm jaw. What was she doing?

"Oh, God," she whispered.

Steve also seemed to wake in the act of pulling her closer. He blinked, and drew back. "What's wrong?"

"You shaved." The words burst past her lips. They came out of nowhere, but the truth of them shocked her even further. "Your beard is gone."

Tension left his body with a long release of air. "Is that all? I thought the bogeyman was right behind me for a minute there." He ran his hand over the contours of his naked face.

"How could you do that?"

Amusement quirked at the corners of his lips. He leaned forward and traced a path down her cheek. "It was easy. Want me to show you what else I can do?"

She slapped his bare shoulder and sat up. Bare shoulder? She skated her gaze down his body. At least he was still wearing his jeans, though they no longer fit the way they were supposed to. She could feel her cheeks flush. She didn't know whether to be relieved or disappointed that he was dressed enough to cover his arousal.

"I didn't know you were going to shave off your beard." To cover her confusion, she made her tone sound almost accusatory. It was bad enough that she was drawn to him when he was a shaggy, rough, lazy bum. Seeing his bared face, she realized that she was in serious trouble. Steven Gregory was downright handsome, and he was anything but a bum.

"I thought you didn't like beards."

"I don't."

Steve reached up and turned on the light next to the bed. Its soft glow illuminated his broad hairy chest for her undisciplined eyes to study. She knew she was staring, but she couldn't help it. There wasn't an ounce of flab on the man. There were, however, a few interesting scars. Interesting? Good grief.

"I have other hair to make up for it," he told her in amusement.

She lifted her gaze from his chest to his naked face and knew that she was blushing again. His face was rugged and compelling, despite the bruise around his eye. Steven Gregory did not have a weak chin or a weak anything else that she could see.

"So I noticed."

"Then what's the problem?" he asked. "Do you want me to shave my chest, too?"

It was the husky tone of his voice and the knowing twinkle in his eyes that got her. Lynn felt additional color rush to her cheeks. She'd been attracted to the bearded bum. She'd been dangerously attracted to the man she'd come to know. But until now, at least, she'd been able to put distance between them with the reminder that she hated hairy faces. Now he was the clean-shaven, potent male she had wanted to kiss witless in this bed, and all she wanted to do was continue where they'd left off. Could she convince herself she hated hairy chests?

Not that one.

She felt highly charged and emotionally drained at the same time. He made her feel wonderful, but her natural caution reared up, waving a red flag.

"I'm not ready for this, Steve."

He rolled onto his side, elbow bent, head resting in the cup of one hand as he watched her through heavy-lidded eyes.

"Ready for what, Lynn?"

"This. Us. You and me." Her gaze swept his length and she really wished it hadn't. She brought it back to his face where it belonged.

A dimple carved a path in his cheek. "Sex?"

He was a devil, pure and simple. Handsome as sin and twice as provocative, even with that small bruise near his left eye. Stretched out on the king-size bed in nothing but a pair of tight jeans, with his hair casually tousled and that flash of dimple when he smiled, he was every woman's fantasy come to life.

From the sitting room came soft, happy baby-type sounds.

"She's probably wet," Lynn said quickly. She scurried off the bed, heart pounding from the erratic flow of blood that rushed through her veins. Steve sat up, his muscled chest an instant draw in the soft light of the room.

"I'll change her and you can get a bottle ready. We don't want her to wake anyone with her cries."

Steve stood and the room shrank. Did he know what she was feeling? Was he still aroused and wanting her? She didn't dare look down to see.

"Lynn, nothing's changed. I just shaved. I'm still me."

"I know." She shoved fingers through her hair. "I know," she repeated more firmly. "I was half-asleep and you surprised me. That's all."

A slow, knowing, masculine smile caused the matching dimple to appear on the other side of his lips. Oh, God, the man was deadly.

"You surprised me, too."

Blood rushed to warm her face again. He knew that she wanted him.

After a moment, his heated look faded, leaving behind a troubled expression. "We're going to have to talk about this attraction sooner or later, Lynn," he said.

She whipped her head up and tried for a smile. "Later."

"Funny, I never took you for a coward."

"See how little you know? I was born with a yellow streak right down the center of my back."

"Oh? I didn't notice it the other night. When you stepped out of the shower, remember?"

She swallowed, but lifted her chin to meet his mocking expression. "Funny. I would have sworn your eyes were elsewhere that night."

His chuckle sent ripples of current through her. She turned and marched out to the sitting room where she began to fuss over the baby.

Steve followed more slowly. She was conscious of his eyes on her before he ambled over and turned on the television. She didn't dare turn around to face him.

Steve flipped through the channels to find a news broadcast. He ran his hand over his smooth cheek and continued to smile. The smile stopped instantly as he saw the story the newscasters were just starting to report. His curse had Lynn spinning around as he turned up the sound.

"...after a bizarre string of incidents this afternoon. It began at this local grocery store." A shot of the grocery story flashed onto the screen.

"Oh, God." Lynn settled the baby back on the couch.

Steve echoed her sentiment as they listened to a mostly factual account of the events of the past few hours. "Police traced that car to a Jerrilynn Rothmore," the commentator continued.

Her knees wouldn't support her slender frame and she sank onto the couch next to the baby as her picture appeared for the entire metropolitan area to see.

"...found her apartment broken into, but no sign of the woman or an infant." There were exterior shots of their apartment house and her car sitting peacefully in the parking lot. The next camera shot was of the pizza parlor. Lynn closed her eyes and groaned.

"You can say that again. They were quicker than I thought." Steve uttered an expletive when the reporter described him pulling a gun and identifying himself as a police officer. Mental visions of his license floating past made him groan.

"The man is described as tall with brown hair and a thick beard. Anyone who has any information relating to this incident is asked to call police at..."

"Now what are we going to do?" she asked, tuning out the next story.

Steve rubbed his face, missing his beard in that moment. "Well, how would you feel about living in Brazil? I don't think we have an extradition treaty with them."

"That's not funny."

"I agree. The climate's too hot. Come on, I bought you some clothing. While you get changed, I'll feed Rachel. We need to get moving."

"Where are we going?"

To her absolute horror, Steve took a pair of scissors to the designer jeans he pulled from one of several shopping bags littering the table. He slashed the jeans open at the knee on one leg and high on the thigh on the other.

"Here."

She took them from his hand, careful not to touch him, which earned her an arrogant smile.

"What did you do that for?"

"Trust me."

"When pigs fly," she muttered.

"I heard that. Here." He handed her a bag. "Get dressed. There's some other things in the sack."

"Are you going to slice them in pieces, too?"

The corners of his eyes crinkled. "Only if you provoke me." Amusement was replaced by a long, silent look. "If you'd rather not get dressed, I can think of something else we can do that doesn't require any clothing at all."

She took the bag and the jeans, awarded him a glare and entered the bathroom. Several minutes of struggle later, she stopped to utter an oath. "I can't wear these. The man is an idiot."

Without warning, Steve opened the door. She stood in the center of the spacious bathroom, trying to snap the jeans closed, to no avail.

"Idiot?"

Heat scalded her cheekbones. "I'm flattered you thought I was a size seven, but even with rigorous dieting, I'm a ten most of the time." That she had managed to wriggle into these jeans was a feat in itself, but she couldn't possibly wear them.

Instead of apologizing, Steve gave a satisfied nod as he surveyed her. His eyes lingered on the snug fit of the pullover. And she knew exactly what he was thinking. Where had he found such a naughty lacy bra? It was exactly the sort of thing she loved to buy for herself. And how had he known her sizes, down to the most intimate detail?

As he continued to look at her with those wanting eyes, she realized she should have donned the baggy sweatshirt that still lay folded on the back of the toilet seat along with the multicolored baseball cap.

His focus traveled down her chest to study the spot where her fingers rested on the partially open zipper. The bikini panties he'd selected didn't come up that high and no amount of tugging brought the shirt down to meet them. His gaze zeroed in on the exposed skin.

"That's great. Just the effect I was after."

The trembling started deep inside her. She hoped he wouldn't notice. "Are you crazy? I can't even button these pants."

"Perfect. Except for that sleekly flat stomach, you look like a woman who just had a baby and is trying to get back into her own clothing."

"And you look like a hungry panther who just spotted dinner." The words burst through her lips without thought.

Steve smiled a slow, seductive smile. "Close, Jerrilynn. I like that panther image."

Darn, but he had a nice smile. "You would. I feel like a kid dressed down for Halloween."

The smile widened. "Maybe so, but there's no way anyone will recognize my yuppie neighbor in this disguise."

She reached for the sweatshirt, holding it in front of her. "This is a disguise?"

He stroked his smooth face, making her yearn to do the same. "What do you think?" Before she could stop him, he reached out and turned her to face the wide expanse of mirror over the sink. He stood so close she could smell that wonderful fragrance again. Oh, blast, her cheeks really were scarlet.

"People will see what they expect to see, Lynn." He rested a hand against her hair, stroking it softly away from her face. "They'll see a loving young couple with their infant daughter." His hand came to rest on her shoulder, branding the skin through the thin pullover. "There are lots of couples with babies, Lynn. Trust me."

"Right. Look where that's gotten me so far."

Hopelessly, helplessly in lust with the wrong man. They did look like the odd couple, but somehow, even that seemed right. She could almost believe they were destined to stay together after this was over.

Just then Rachel let out a cry, effectively breaking the spell.

The dimples became more pronounced. "Hey, it's not so bad. We aren't in jail yet."

"Thanks," she said with a liberal dose of sarcasm. "I needed you to remind me."

His grin was wicked, and he reached out to plop the baseball cap on her head. "Personally, I think you look terrific. Not like a yuppie at all."

"You would." She fingered the cap, then slanted him a sly expression. He, too, had changed clothes while she had been in the bathroom. And the change was alarming to every sense she possessed. "Maybe I don't look like a yuppie, but you do."

For just a moment, Steve appeared startled and then he looked down at himself and began to laugh. It was a deep hearty chuckle that demanded a response from her. She couldn't help thinking that he did look totally different now, and not just because of his denuded face. His new clothes would not be amiss on any one of her male acquaintances. It was very much in tune with the yuppie look Steve derided, yet Steve wore that clothing as if it had been designed with him in mind.

Sitting in the car a short time later, Lynn pondered the dramatic turn her life had taken since Steve came pelting into it. All those self-doubts about what she wanted from life seemed to have crystallized into a new definition of success. One that had nothing to do with work and everything to do with children and a family.

She was still smiling to herself when Steve pulled into a shopping center and parked near a pay phone. As if he'd been inside her thoughts, he said, "Wait here, little mama. I'll be right back."

The phrase sent a tingle of pleasure along her nerve endings. Only too well could Lynn imagine being a mother. The mother of Steve's child. And that was the scariest thought of all. Steven Gregory turned her on in a way that no other man ever had. Was the attraction simply due to proximity and the crazy situation in which they currently found themselves?

Through the car window, she watched Steve's lithe stride as he crossed the sidewalk, approached the pay phone, inserted a coin and dialed a number.

Tim answered on the first ring. "My God, man, where the hell are you? Never mind," he said, taking a breath. "I'm not sure I want to know. Geez, buddy, you're hotter than molten lava. You made the six-o'clock news. Or at least your sidekick did. I assume you were the bearded man."

"Afraid so," Steve confirmed glumly. "I'm surprised they didn't release my name, too."

Tim swore. "Didn't I tell you to get rid of that baby?"

"I tried."

There was a beat of silence. "Okay. What's going down and how can I help?"

As succinctly as possible, Steve gave him the highlights. "Basically, I need information."

"Give me some names."

"Barrett and Alice Montgomery. I need to know why Lynn's sister, Marcy, had their child in the first place."

"What does Lynn think?"

Steve looked over at the car. Lynn watched him intently, too far away to overhear his conversation. "She doesn't seem to have a clue."

"Could she be protecting Marcy?"

Steve studied the numerals on the telephone pad. It had never occurred to him, but it was a good question. He hadn't shown Lynn the drugs yet. Would she protect Marcy at all costs? He gave a mental snort. Of course she would protect her sister, but not at all costs.

"I don't know much about Marcy, except that she's the youngest in the family, and spoiled as well as irresponsible. I don't know what she does to support herself—when she isn't kidnapping babies."

"I don't like the sound of this, Steve."

"Me, neither, and you don't know the worst part."

"It gets worse?"

"I don't think Alice Montgomery left her house voluntarily. There's blood and a bloody knife on her kitchen floor."

Tim uttered a word that about summed up the situation. "You said she isn't even a redhead," Tim complained.

Steve's lips twitched at the reference to his well-known preference for red-haired women.

"I've decided they're overrated."

There was a moment of silence. "Yeah. I was getting that impression from you myself."

Even with his friend, Steve couldn't bring himself to discuss Lynn. He wasn't sure what he was feeling for her. "Listen, I'd appreciate whatever information you can get on the Montgomerys."

"All right. Anyone else?"

Steve let out a pent-up breath. They couldn't afford to ignore anything or anyone until they found out what was going on. Besides, if Steve was lucky, Lynn would never know they were looking into her family.

"Lynn has a brother and parents, as well as her sister," he told Tim, still a bit reluctantly. "The brother is supposed to be in England on business and the parents are overseas touring. Australia, I think she said."

"Easy enough to check. What about Lynn?"

"She's an accountant with Morely, Abelman, Jacks and Varney. She's supposed to be either in California or on her way back right now. The airline screwed up her tickets, so she decided to skip the meeting rather than go late. There's a boyfriend." He heard Tim draw in a breath of surprise. "David somebody. I don't think he figures in. I get the impression it's a one-sided sort of thing. She doesn't seem to like him all that much." He hoped. "Besides, I don't recall seeing any men's clothing in her closets." Despite the possessive way David-the-dork talked to her answering machine.

Steve could almost picture Tim pushing his long square fingers through his sandy brown hair. "Okay. What else can I do right now?"

Steve flipped through the telephone directory in front of him as they talked. He stopped on the page marked Hospitals. "Tell the cops what a fine, upstanding employee I am?"

"You want me to lie?" Then, more seriously, Tim asked, "What did you do with the drugs and the jewelry?"

"They're in the bottom of the diaper bag."

"Don't you think you should get rid of them?"

"Yeah, but I'd really like to do it so Kevin takes a fall."

"Risky, Steve, real risky."

"I know. Could you have some bail money handy? By the way, you'd better have someone meet your brother's plane when it comes in. I don't think we want him driving around in my truck when the police and other unfriendlies have it identified."

"Good point. What are you going to do now?"

Steve put his mind back on business. "Check out the phone call about the motorcar accident."

"Motorcar?"

"He was British."

"Didn't you just say the Rothmore brother is in England on business?"

Steve stopped, his mind sifting through that bit of information, trying to see where, if at all, it fit. He looked back over at the car. "Yeah," he said slowly. "That's what she told me."

Tim made a sound that could have been a hiss. "Well, it could be coincidence."

Steve hated coincidences. He had never once considered that Lynn might be involved in this mess any further than he was himself. Was it possible that he was playing the role of dupe? The idea unsettled him almost as much as that scene in the bedroom earlier.

"Steve, you'd better be prepared for anything," Tim warned.

"Yeah. I'll keep the agency out of it, Tim. I promise."

"Hey, I wasn't worried about that. Just stay safe. And watch your back, buddy. I really don't like the sound of this."

Lynn continued to stare at him from wide anxious eyes. Could she be involved? Was she that good an actress? He turned away. "Yeah. I know just what you mean."

"Before you hang up—Jack Price called and left a message. He said to tell you the license is still valid and in his name. He's willing to sell it at the price you discussed, if you're still interested."

Excitement coursed through Steve. The license was the key to his future. A future that had nothing to do with being a private investigator.

"Does this mean we're going to lose you?" Tim asked.

"Not for a while, unless I get my investigator's license yanked as a result of this fiasco. Did Jack leave a number?"

"Hey, don't worry about that. We're not going to let that happen, and yes, he did leave a number."

Steve hung up a few minutes later and jotted down several more phone numbers before he closed the telephone book. He tried to call Jack Price, but the man wasn't home. Steve told himself he needed to control his excitement and deal with the immediate situation first. The land and the license would wait. He strode back to the car, his gaze fastened on Lynn.

"What did you find out?" she asked as he slid inside. "Is something else wrong?"

"That depends. What do you know that you haven't told me?" he asked softly.

She blinked, her face blank. "What are you talking about?"

"Who is Bob Haskell?"

"I haven't a clue." Unease put a break in her voice, but she still looked only confused.

He hated this, but he had to be absolutely sure. "That's what I want to know. He's the one who made the telephone call to Alice Montgomery."

"I remember. Just what exactly did your boss have to say, Steve? This is beginning to sound like an inquisition."

"Answer the question, Lynn," he said, determined to hear it from her lips, even though her body language had already told him what he wanted to know.

Her sudden sense of betrayal was worse than anything she had experienced so far. Was she falling in love with a man who didn't trust her?

"I don't think so," she said quietly, with all the dignity she could muster. "*Trust me.* Isn't that your favorite phrase?"

She reached for the seat belt and unsnapped it. Her hand was on the door handle when he grabbed her other arm.

"Where do you think you're going?"

"To the police," she snapped. "Just like you wanted to do in the first place. I don't like playing games. Particularly not games where I don't know the rules."

"Neither do I." He released her arm but not her gaze. "I'm sorry. Will you give me a chance to explain?"

"Like you just gave me?"

He sat back and rubbed his jaw. "You told me your brother is in England on business."

"What does that have to do with anything?"

"Not one damn thing," he admitted ruefully. "But for a minute there, I did wonder if you were stringing me along for reasons of your own."

"Stringing you along?" Her voice was hoarse with disbelief. "How? About what?"

He shook his head. "I don't know."

She waited, but he didn't say any more. "You don't know. That's it? You come back to the car with crazy questions because my brother is in England?"

"When you put it that way, it does sound pretty weak, but you have to admit, we've got an awful lot going on that seems to tie back to England."

"So?" Angry sparks flashed like lightning from her storm-laden eyes. "You..." She froze, her entire face awash in dread. Steve pivoted and saw the police car pulling into the shopping center. His own heart thudded erratically.

Without hesitating, he spanned the distance between them and captured her chin, bringing her face around to him. With his fingers laced in her hair, he tugged her close enough for their lips to touch. Instead of kissing her, he spoke quietly, with subtle force. "Put your seat belt on and keep talking to me. No. Don't look at them. Keep looking at me."

He released her, and almost mechanically her fingers fumbled for the belt. "Keep facing me and start talking. Smile if you can, and don't look at the police car."

Her smile was as helpless as a two-hour-old kitten, but it was there. The woman had guts, he thought again. "What am I supposed to talk about? If he recognizes us..."

Steve threw back his head and forced a laugh, sending the car rolling forward. He split his attention between her and the other cars moving through the parking lot. Lynn glared as if he'd lost his mind.

"You're doing great," he told her. "He can't possibly recognize you. Why would he? He can't see the baby, I don't have a beard, and we aren't driving around in a pickup truck."

"You're really a beast, you know that, Gregory? You're enjoying this, aren't you? Admit it. I'm scared to death and you're having a ball."

The police car passed them as they were waiting in line to turn out of the shopping center. Steve began to breathe more easily. Lynn never even noticed. "Why did Marcy have to knock on your door? There are probably over a hundred people in that building. What did I do to deserve you?"

"Cheer up, sweetheart. It's a building full of yuppies. No doubt I was the only person at home in the entire complex at that hour of the day."

"That's another thing. If it's such a yuppie haven and you disdain anything to do with them, then what are you doing living in that building?"

Steve swallowed a chuckle. He knew it was rotten, but he loved to see her all riled up like this. There was a lot of fire under those business suits. Did anyone suspect? Did David-the-dork know how spectacular she was beneath her prim veneer?

"I like living there. It's close to work, and watching everyone in their daily uniform driving their BMWs serves to remind me on a regular basis of what I don't want to turn into."

Before she could tear another strip off him, Steve turned the car into the hotel parking lot. That caused her to sit up and look around. "What are we doing back here?"

"I'm going to drop you and the baby off while I check out a couple of hospitals. You can order some dinner from room service. It should be safe."

"No."

"What do you mean, no?"

"It's a simple word, Steve. It means I'm not going to sit around waiting for the police to show up and arrest me for kidnapping and God alone knows what else. No means I am coming with you."

His lips twitched, but he held on to the grin. "I thought you hated this. I thought you were terrified."

"I am, but it's a question of choosing between two evils. You're at least one step up from the man who grabbed me in the rest room, and entire heads above Kevin."

"Gee, thanks."

"What if someone else with a British accent comes along while the baby and I are alone?"

The urge to smile was gone. "It won't happen."

"What if Kevin finds me?"

Steve looked grim. "Not a chance."

"You don't know that."

She was right. He hadn't yet told her about finding the drugs in Marcy's car. There was a slim possibility that Kevin knew exactly where they were and was just biding his time.

Her jaw set. "The last time you left us alone, I was kidnapped and shot at. I'll take my chances with you."

It took them three phone calls to locate Barrett Montgomery.

Steve replaced the receiver. "Intensive care. Damn."

"At least we found him. Now maybe we can get to the bottom of little Rachel's abandonment."

Steve let his fingers drum against the hub of the steering wheel. "Lynn, we won't be able to get in to see him. They only let immediate family inside."

"So? My dear brother may be dying."

"He's British."

She crossed her arms over her chest and gave him a smug look. "We'll just have to fake it, don't you know, old chap," she said with perfect British haughtiness.

Chapter Eight

"He keeps calling for his wife, poor man." The nurse peered down at the patient in the bed. Tubes sprouted from a variety of places where tubes were never meant to go. For such a large man, he looked small and shrunken against the white hospital sheets.

"It's a good thing he doesn't really know where he is or what's happening," the aide responded with pity. He was supposed to be a good-looking man, but the parts not covered in bruises and cuts were covered in bandages.

The man stirred slightly. He muttered restlessly, the name he called barely understandable. The aide turned away from his pain. With a last look at the monitors, the nurse accompanied her from the room.

"I heard the police think he was forced off the road."

The nurse frowned, looked around, and seeing no one nearby, lowered her voice. "Uh-huh. His car rolled down an embankment. There wasn't much left, from what I hear. Probably some drunk driver who doesn't even remember what happened. They're looking for a light blue car. If that poor man dies, it will be murder."

IT WAS TOO LATE to drive to the hospital, they decided. Morning would be soon enough and by then, with any luck, Rachel's father might even be transferred from intensive care. Steve offered to pick up Chinese take-out, and, as the restaurant was only a few blocks away, Lynn was quick to agree.

He returned to the warm hotel room to find Rachel asleep in the middle of the remade bed and every light in the suite shining brightly. On a purely masculine level, Steve was glad Lynn was aware of him in a sexual way. He turned off the bedroom light and shut the door. Lynn set out the spicy food and sat down.

She had removed her sweatshirt, and Steve found himself envious of her T-shirt. The tight fabric molded every curve. He wished he hadn't ordered hot and spicy. It was overkill with Lynn sitting across from him.

Between bites of food and neutral conversation, Steve studied her. Based on her heightened color and the nervous way she avoided his eyes, he knew she was aware that he was looking at her. At a guess, she was sorry she had taken off the sweatshirt. He kept thinking about the wisp of a lacy bra he had purchased and he wondered if she was wearing it underneath that shirt.

Despite lines of fatigue and a faint bruise on her cheek, she stirred a primitive need in him. He watched her take a bite of food and chew slowly, pausing to lick a trace of plum sauce from her lip.

Steve managed not to groan out loud. He really wanted to be the one doing the licking. She was driving him insane and she had no idea. Absently, he rubbed his aching shoulder.

Lynn set down her plastic fork on the paper plate and pushed it to one side. "What's wrong?"

"With what?"

"Just now, you looked like you were in pain, and now you're rubbing your shoulder. What's wrong with it?"

Steve dropped his hand. He couldn't tell her the two actions weren't connected.

Her eyes narrowed suspiciously. "Did you get hurt when you were fighting with Kevin?"

"No. It's nothing."

Her lips pursed. "Right. Nothing. Let me see what you've done." She rose and came around the table.

"Really, Lynn, it's fine." If she touched him right now, he wasn't going to be responsible. "I wrenched it this afternoon when I heard the gunshots." He pushed his own chair away from the table.

Her eyes darkened, but she was undeterred. "And when did you hurt your knee? Don't look so surprised. You were limping when you got back here with the food."

"I was not limping."

Her look scolded him.

"Okay, maybe I was favoring it," he said ruefully, "but I was not limping." She walked around to stand behind him and he felt her hands close over his shoulders. "What are you doing?"

"Hold still and stop being such a baby. My dad gets bursitis and he says I have magic fingers."

Steve swallowed his immediate response as her supple fingers began to knead the tight muscles in his shoulders. Her action shouldn't have had any sexual connotations whatsoever, but it only helped to tighten an entirely different set of muscles. He could smell the light clean fragrance that clung to her clothing. It would take a more noble man than he to tell her to stop.

"Your dad is right," he told her after a minute. "You do have magic fingers."

"So this is helping?"

Steve bit his lip. "Mmm."

"Steve?" Her voice was hesitant and her fingers paused. "What are we going to do about tonight?"

"Tonight?" He lifted his head then quickly lowered it. "Don't stop. What do you mean, what are we going to do about tonight?" He knew exactly what she meant. "We're going to get some sleep. It's too late to do much else."

"I know, but there's only one bed. If you sleep on the couch, where is the baby going to sleep? I'm not used to sleeping with anyone," she rushed on. "I might roll over and squish her or something."

He caught her expression in the mirror across from them. Sure enough, her face was a delicate shade of pink. Surreptitiously, he watched her bite down on her lower lip.

"What makes you think I plan to sleep on the couch?"

Lynn's hands stopped moving altogether. She rested them on his shoulders and he could feel her warmth through the shirt he wore.

"Oh. Of course. Sorry. It only makes sense for me to take the couch. I'm shorter. I wasn't—"

"The baby is even shorter than you are. Why is it I have a feeling you're going to object to giving Rachel the couch and letting us share the bed? I'd be willing to let you squish me." In more ways than one. He remembered every lush curve on her glorious body. Somehow, Steve didn't think now was the time to tell her that.

In the mirror, he watched the pink deepen. Still, he thought he detected a sparkle of—interest? desire? excitement?—something in her fathomless gray eyes. She looked down before he could be sure.

"Don't be silly."

"Trust me, humor was not my intent." He shrugged easily. "Hey, I'm not used to sleeping with anyone, either." Not that it didn't hold a whole lot of appeal if that anyone was her.

"Yeah, right."

"You saw my place," he protested.

Her eyes softened to a warm cashmere and the fingers started moving again in broad strokes that stopped just short of being a caress. What brought that expression to her face? Certainly not his junkyard furnishings.

"So what are we going to do?" she asked.

He knew Lynn was fighting their attraction. What he didn't know was why. Unless David-the-dork was more important to her than he thought.

"Well, I still say we could share the bed. You and this David person aren't serious, are you?"

Lynn blinked in surprise. Her smile came with a quick toss of her head. "I guess you could say he is. David Linnington takes everything seriously. He lives in our building on the top floor. We leave for work about the same time every morning. I made the mistake of going out with him a couple of times. Once was enough, but—"

Steve leaned back and tried not to look smug. "David-the-dork doesn't take hints, does he?"

She tried to look severe, but a giggle broke free. "Not even if you use a two-by-four."

"Next time, try a herd of stampeding elephants."

"I don't think so," she replied. "Cruelty to animals."

Their eyes met in shared laughter and held in the mirror across the room. He liked that she didn't turn away. More and more, he was coming to admire this woman.

Her breathing quickened. So did his. "Would I be totally out of line if I tell you that you have glorious skin—in addition to magic fingers?"

Her fingers resumed their kneading more quickly. "I don't think it's a good idea."

Hell, he knew that. Unless she wanted him as much as he wanted her? Her mouth parted slightly and her fingers stopped again, almost as if she'd heard his thought. Her long thick lashes partially obscured her eyes—smoky bedroom eyes. He pivoted in the chair to grasp her hips. A soft sound escaped her.

"Why isn't it a good idea?"

She didn't answer, but she didn't resist when he tugged her forward to stand between his thighs. "I won't do anything you don't want me to do, Jerrilynn. That's a promise." His eyes pinned her where she stood.

"That's not much of a promise."

His pulse went into overdrive. Her voice was shaky, but she regarded him steadily as she reached out to brace her hands against his shoulders. He caught a glimpse of white teeth as she bit down on her lower lip and swallowed. Fine tremors traversed her body and he knew then, she wanted him. He shifted, glad for the loose linen slacks he was wearing instead of his usual jeans.

He slid his fingers along her hips in a sensual caress against the tight denims she wore. A pulse beat rapidly in her throat as she stared down at him, but she made no move to pull away.

On impulse, he stretched forward. Her gasp echoed in his ears as his mouth suddenly covered her left nipple through the fabric of the T-shirt. He sucked at the tip and she clenched his shoulders and threw back her head. He closed his other hand around her right breast to massage the distended tip through the material.

"Steve." It was almost a moan.

She didn't pull away so he allowed his fingers to slide upward. The shirt pulled free from the waistband of her pants, exposing the flat expanse of her midriff above the unclosed zipper. His body went crazy. He pressed his thumbs against her ribs just beneath the swell of her breasts. He tugged her closer into the cradle of him, watching as her eyes widened in awareness and her breathing caught in her throat.

The deciding factor was that she didn't move back or try to step away. "I promise. Nothing you don't want too, Lynn. All you have to do is say no."

Their eyes locked. He hardened in anticipation. "Kiss me."

The words hovered in the air between them.

Slowly, she cupped his face. Her head descended to within inches of his mouth. He could taste her breath against his lips. Then she darted her tongue forward to skim across his lips, to outline them in careful deliberation. His mouth parted in surprise. It took effort not to draw her forward and seal them in a kiss, but he was determined to let her set the pace, even if she killed him with slow torture.

She drew his bottom lip forward and sucked lightly on the fullness there. He swallowed another groan.

And then her lips covered his in a kiss as sweet and as golden as warm honey.

Her eyes were closed and a soft sound escaped her lips. Her hands bunched and then smoothed the material of his shirt. "You're making me crazy," she accused quietly. Her eyes opened to lock again with his.

"Good," he said hoarsely. This time, his mouth closed over the other breast. She moved forward against the cradle of his body and a tiny moan escaped her lips. One hand reached up to stroke his hair.

"Steve..."

"Take off your shirt for me."

Her eyes sprang open.

"You're so sexy and you don't even seem to know it—until a man gets a glimpse of that erotic underwear you favor. That's when he suspects you know your power as a woman. It's exciting to think of what you hide under all that control."

Her eyes sparkled with heated excitement. The tip of her tongue danced across her lips. Steve skimmed the taut skin of her sides with his fingers, stopping just beneath her breasts. Slowly, he slid a finger beneath the lacy cup to rub the hardened nipple. His body sang at the touch.

A whimper of sound crossed her lips. "There's hidden heat inside you, Lynn. If you turn it loose, we'll probably set the hotel on fire."

The pulse beat more rapidly in her throat. Steve had the strongest desire to lick that pulse point and soothe it with kisses. He released her and brought his hands up so the palms faced her, scant millimeters from the hardened nipples beneath the thin layer of cloth. If she breathed any deeper, he would be touching her.

"Take off your shirt, Lynn."

The next move had to be hers. It might kill him if she backed away now, but it had to be her choice. Had he ever wanted a woman this badly?

Slowly, Lynn held his eyes and raised the hem of the T-shirt, up and over her head.

"Thank God."

Lynn almost smiled at his relief. His expression was immediately replaced by a sexual hunger so unbridled she felt it like a physical caress. She wanted him. Both the fierce panther and the compassionate hero who comprised both sides of this complex man. Her fingers went to the front clasp of her bra.

"Hurry."

His husky plea warmed her blood. Blood that was already stirred by a primal need for this man. Still, she forced her fingers to move slowly. To prolong this sexual game he had started. She'd never done such a thing before. Never before wanted to do the sorts of things that were occurring to her fevered imagination. His eyes narrowed to glittery slits as the cups of the lacy material parted and her breasts spilled forth, the nipples still hard.

"Beautiful." It was almost a sigh. He pushed aside the material and cupped her breasts with his hands. The contact brought another soft moan to her lips.

"See how perfectly they fit?"

She couldn't take a deep breath. Low in her belly was a fevered tingle that only he could assuage. As he drew one nipple into his mouth and sucked, the contact of his moist mouth against her skin nearly sent her over the precipice.

"So beautiful. So responsive."

His fingers fumbled at the opened zipper of her jeans. She reciprocated by freeing the buttons on his shirt. He was all hard planes and rippling muscles and lusciously soft dark hair, as strong and beautiful as she remembered. The tiny nubs of his nipples responded immediately to the flick of her touch. She parted the whorls of hair, and it was his turn to moan as she bent and licked each stony point.

The sound thrilled her.

Rachel began to cry.

They froze. The cry rose in volume. As one, their heads swiveled toward the closed door. "Maybe she'll go back to sleep."

Steve looked at her and shut his eyes, his expression pained. "Want to bet?"

He was right.

Lynn reached for the discarded T-shirt, only to blush at the wet marks. She put it back down and slipped on the sweatshirt, instead. Steve hurried to button his shirt. She didn't have the heart to tell him he skipped a button as he rushed into the bedroom. He looked every inch a desirable man, tousled and sexy as hell.

She got out a can of formula and a bottle. She could hear Steve in the other room, talking to the crying infant.

"Your timing is rotten, kid," Steve told Rachel. "Just wait until you're sixteen and some young stud is trying to kiss you on the front porch."

Lynn chuckled. She could actually picture the scene. No one would mess with his daughter when Steve was around.

"Good thing Lynn put that extra blanket under you. I told you that you weren't big enough to contain this much liquid. Where do you store it all? We're going to have to find a Laundromat, at this rate."

Rachel's wails grew in volume. Lynn stepped inside with the bottle and Steve offered her a slow smile. A smile that had nothing to do with babies and everything to do with the two of them.

"Hold that thought," he told her, stroking the backs of her fingers as he took the bottle from her hand.

Rachel didn't want another bottle and she wasn't the least bit sleepy. She was, however, fussy and demanding. They took turns walking her, to no avail.

"Do you think she's sick? Maybe we should take her to the hospital."

Steve frowned, jiggling his small burden. "Tim and Petey's little girl used to act like this at times. I never appreciated all those dark circles under his eyes before. I think I owe him an apology for all the teasing."

"She's been crying a long time now," Lynn protested.

"It's only been ten minutes, Lynn. We'll give it another half hour. If she doesn't stop by then, I'll call Petey. Why don't you lie down and get some rest?" he offered. "No need for both of us to pace."

"Like I could sleep with Rachel so upset?" But Lynn did sit down on the couch. She was tired. If only the baby felt the same.

"You know, kid, somebody is going to have to teach you the difference between morning and evening. You've got your hours completely screwed up."

A short time later, Steve rubbed his tired eyes and turned to Lynn. She was sound asleep, her head tilted against the back of the couch, exposing the long line of her throat. The strange protectiveness he experienced was new. The feeling surprised him because he had plans, and they didn't include a yuppie wife who traveled all the time and was locked into a demanding career.

He set the now-quiet baby in her carrier and bent to rouse Lynn. She came partially awake and grumpily allowed him to steer her toward the bedroom. He didn't dare leave Rachel alone for more than a few seconds for fear she'd start fussing again.

He closed the door, thankful the baby was in a better humor for the moment. He wished he was. "How does anyone manage to have more than one child?" he asked the baby. She gurgled in response.

Since it was obvious he wasn't going to get any sleep for a while, he decided to return Jack Price's call. With the baby settled in his arms, he made a deal that would ensure the future he had been dreaming of for some time.

He got off the phone, excitement singing through his veins, and looked at the closed bedroom door. Restlessly, he got up and began to pace, playing with the baby. He wanted to share this news with someone.

No, not someone, he realized. With Lynn.

He didn't have the heart to wake her. The news would keep. He closed his eyes, then rubbed them. Even the excitement generated by Jack Price wasn't enough. He needed sleep. The way events were unfolding, he needed to be rested for whatever the next day was apt to bring. At their current rate, that could be just about anything.

IT WAS EARLY MORNING, but the intensive care unit took no notice of time. People came and went in a steady stream, but every one of them was cleared through a set of double doors and an intercom system. No one simply walked in.

Still, there were ways inside. A person only had to be smart and brazen and choose carefully. It wouldn't be so very difficult, after all. Only, why hadn't he had the decency to die in the car wreck? He should have, damn his soul.

No, what he should have done was come across with the money. In the end, he would, anyhow—one way or another. He lay in that hospital bed surrounded by machines designed to keep him alive. They wouldn't protect him. Nothing would. It was too bad he hadn't had the sense to die the first time.

And once he was dead, something could be done about the baby. That stupid girl would pay for taking the child. She had nearly ruined everything. But it wouldn't matter. After he was dead, the girl would follow. Then something would have to be done with the baby. Maybe she could be bartered for even more lovely money. It was an invigorating thought.

THEY SAT in a corner booth at the noisy fast-food restaurant, eating a late breakfast. Looking at Steve, Lynn wondered if the same lines of fatigue etched both their faces. The baby gurgled happily.

"How can people have more than one kid?" Steve asked.

Lynn smothered a yawn. "When do they have time to have a second one?"

Their eyes met and held. They hadn't had to worry about sharing a bed last night. Rachel had seen to that. She was up every two hours like clockwork, leaving Lynn and Steve too exhausted to do more than trade places as they took turns walking with her in the living room of the suite.

All morning, their conversation had been stilted. Memories of what had almost happened never lay far from Lynn's thoughts. She watched Steve's handsome profile as he took a quick glance around for the third time. No one sat anywhere near their table. At the moment, a young woman with three small children was their closest neighbor. Steve asked Lynn for the diaper bag and dug to the bottom of it. He removed a white-and-red drugstore bag that she hadn't noticed before.

"What's that?"

He had such strong, capable hands.

"Look inside."

Reflexively, Lynn took the package. She studied his expression and made no move to open it. "What is it?"

"Open the bag."

Lynn didn't want to look in the bag. Instinct told her that once she did, everything would change again. Reluctantly, she glanced inside.

"My necklace? My earrings! And this is Grandma's brooch, but I don't recognize the rest of these pieces." Her fingers moved through the bits of jewelry and she raised her eyes. "Where did you get them?"

"Finish looking," he told her gruffly.

She fingered past the jewelry and touched the bottles. Her eyes were shadowed as she raised them to meet Steve's. Slowly, she pulled out one of the two prescription bottles and read the label. "Penicillin?"

Steve spanned the table with one arm and removed the bottle from her hand. He opened it and discreetly shook two pills into his palm. "Amphetamines," he corrected. "Enough here to give a number of addicts a real high for some time."

She stared at him blankly. "I don't understand. You mean Kevin is an addict?"

"I found all of this—the drugs, the jewelry, all of it—in Marcy's car. Marcy's, not Kevin's."

"No." The word was uttered with complete certainty.

As though she hadn't spoken, Steve returned the pills to the container and screwed down the cap. The bottle disappeared inside the bag. "Maybe they belong to Kevin, but you need to face the possibility that they may also belong to your sister."

His eyes refused to release hers as he continued deliberately. "Taken with the jewelry, I'd say either one, or both of them, has a serious habit. Or else they're selling drugs to people who do."

"No." This time, the word was a frozen puff of sound in the noisy room.

He placed the sack back into the deepest part of the diaper bag. "Wishing won't make it so. If your sister is doing drugs, there will be signs. Symptoms you can't help noticing. Bouts of jittery, almost-hyperactivity, followed by periods of depression. Severe mood swings, even paranoia and hallucinations aren't uncommon signs."

This time, the N-word wouldn't come. This time, the trepidation charged through her body in slick waves that wouldn't be denied. Because lately, since Marcy had taken up with Kevin, her mood swings had become very pronounced. Several times, Lynn thought it was because her sister was drinking too much. The night of Lynn's party was a perfect example. Lynn closed her eyes and felt Steve's hand close over her own.

"We need to find her, Lynn. Tim's absolutely right. Your sister is the key to everything."

Lynn looked at him with hope. "Maybe she took the bag from Kevin. She was probably going to return the jewelry to me."

It was too much like pulling wings off a butterfly to say what he really believed. "Maybe."

Her chin lifted fractionally. "Of course she was. Why else would she have them? She would never steal from me."

Steve gritted his teeth and choked back his initial response. He settled for a deep sigh. "I hope you're right."

"Of course I'm right. Damn that girl. I'm going to wring her neck when I see her."

"Get in line. What are the chances you'd go back to the hotel and wait while I check out the hospital?"

Lynn pasted a sweet smile on her lips. "On a scale of one to ten, try zero."

"That's what I thought," he muttered.

"Until we get hold of my sister or locate Rachel's parents, you and I are going to be nearly inseparable."

"I like the sounds of that."

Lynn tried to ignore the mischief in his eyes and those heart-stopping dimples. Even though neither of them had mentioned last night's interrupted scene, she knew he hadn't forgotten any more than she had. She also knew it was only a matter of time before the scene had a different ending.

"You do understand that only immediate family members can get inside intensive care," he reminded her. "There is no way they'll let a baby in there."

Lynn raised an eyebrow. "Are you planning to ask me to wait in the car again?"

"Not me, lady. I learned my lesson. On the other hand, how would you feel about sitting in the lobby?"

"I hope you're kidding. I'm the one with the accent, remember, old chap?"

Steve sighed. "Since we're not going to get inside to see him, anyhow, I guess it won't matter if you come up with me."

"Why—"

"The man won't be in any shape for questions. I just want to talk to someone on staff about his condition and prognosis, and maybe about his wife if I can find a chatty nurse."

"Oh."

First, they stopped while Steve called Tim. Against his better judgment, Steve let the phone in Tim's private office ring until it transferred to Theresa. Only, she didn't answer, either. After the third ring, he hung up before the answering service could cut in. Had Tim gotten smart and fired Theresa, or had she finally given up and quit? He didn't really care, but someone should be picking up. He decided to try Tim at home, but there was no answer at the house, either.

Perplexed, Steve glared at the telephone as if it were personally responsible for his problem. Reinserting the quarter, he tried Tim's car phone. When it rang unanswered, he slammed down the phone and stalked back to the car. Where the devil was everyone?

"What's wrong now?" Lynn asked as he slid behind the wheel.

He frowned, trying to curb his annoyance. "Tim's not answering."

"Well, it is Saturday morning," she said reasonably. "Did you try him at home?"

"Saturday?" His astonished expression was comical. "What happened to Friday?"

Lynn smiled and chucked the baby under the chin. "He's losing it, kid." Rachel gurgled happy agreement.

"Don't listen to her, Rachel. I've had a hard week."

Lynn's smile widened. "Poor baby. So now what?"

Steve shrugged. "I guess we might as well go over to the hospital. Any idea what time visiting hours start?"

"Probably around nine."

"It's after that now."

"We had a late breakfast," she reminded him.

Visiting hours were in full swing when they finally reached the sprawling brick building. The visitors' parking lot in front of the main entrance was close to full. A lot of people were walking around both inside and out. No one paid any attention to the couple with the tiny baby, except to throw them an occasional smile. Since this was a hospital, even Steve's lightly bruised face didn't draw any undue notice.

The elevators seemed ponderously slow as they waited. Then they had to step back to let a large group disembark before they could get inside. As luck would have it, they were the only two people going up from the main lobby.

Steve stared straight ahead as the elevator doors closed, trying to plan his strategy. Because he wasn't paying attention, it took several long seconds for the face to register.

"Wait!" The doors slid shut and the elevator began to climb. Frantically, Steve pressed the button for two.

"What are you doing? We need to go—"

"Barrett Montgomery," he interrupted. "I just saw a man who resembled him."

"Rachel's father? But he's in intensive care."

"Yes, I know." He reached to pull at his beard, found it missing and settled for scratching his chin, instead. "It could have been a relative."

"Are you sure?"

"No, damn it, I didn't get a clear view. He reminded me of the picture I saw." The elevator opened and Steve stepped out as an orderly with a gurney stepped in. "I'll meet you upstairs. Wait for me."

"Hey, wait a minute." But three more people squeezed past to step inside and the doors closed before Lynn could follow him out.

Steve looked around until he spotted the stairwell. He'd been wrong, of course. Barrett Montgomery, in the picture on the bedroom dresser, had thick wavy auburn hair. The man hurrying past the elevators had short red hair and glasses. Steve had an eye for detail and his instincts were seldom wrong. But it was only a glimpse. He could have been mistaken. Or, hopefully, it was a relative.

Could it be, after all, that Marcy really was supposed to be baby-sitting while Barrett Montgomery was in intensive care? But in that case, where was Marcy? And who was after the baby?

Footsteps thundered down the metal stairs from above him. Heavy, running steps that sounded like more than one set of feet. Steve reached the main level and stopped. Security staff was everywhere. Even as he surveyed the scene, the door behind him swung open, almost hitting him in the back as two more security people charged from the stairwell.

"Excuse me," one of the men said. The other, an older man, paused to study him. He stared hard at Steve's slightly blackened eye. "Did you just come down those stairs?" he asked.

"Yes, sir," Steve responded promptly. His heart accelerated. "Is something wrong?"

"What floor were you coming from?"

"The second."

The man frowned, but apparently, Steve didn't match the description of whoever they were chasing. Yet, the guard hadn't missed Steve's black eye or his scraped hand. It took a real effort on Steve's part to keep from putting his bruised knuckles behind his back like a naughty child.

"Did you see or hear anyone else on the stairs?" the man asked.

"Just someone running down behind me. I assume that was you." He tried to appear relaxed and only mildly curious, but his mind turned to Lynn and a diaper bag full of amphetamines. "Is something wrong?"

The guard merely shook his head and hurried after his partner. Steve followed more slowly to the front of the building and stopped. A county police cruiser pulled up, and he could see security people fanning out over the parking lot. There were people everywhere, but no sign of the man he had glimpsed on the elevator. This didn't look like a particularly good time to go wandering around trying to find him, either.

Annoyed, yet curious, Steve paused to observe the scene for a few minutes. When two more police cars pulled up, he decided he had pushed his luck far enough and turned to go back inside.

Just then, Lynn stepped from an elevator amid a crush of people waiting to get on. Her eyes fairly sparkled with excitement. A large, boisterous group of well-wishers bearing balloons entered the lobby at the same time as a group of nurses exited the other elevator. The lobby looked like Grand Central Station.

Steve tried to pull Lynn aside, away from the crowd, but she shook her head, refusing to be led. There was little choice but to make a scene or follow her outside. She allowed him to take the heavy baby carrier from her. Rachel smiled happily.

He followed her, his mind on the drugstore packet buried inside the diaper bag she carried. If they were stopped now, it would take a good lawyer to get them out of police hands. Tim would not be pleased.

Lynn hesitated briefly when she saw the police cars and security men milling about, but then she turned toward Steve and began a stream of steady chatter as they strode past the nearest officer, with a group of nurses right behind them.

"Didn't Aunt Martha look terrific? I'm so glad she's feeling better. She was so happy to see the baby. It's too bad our daughter was so cranky." The innocent baby smiled up at them from the carrier.

"I told you she wouldn't be upset by your bruises," Lynn went on. Steve wondered if she had caught the look the policeman shot them. "Did you hear that they might let her come home tomorrow or Monday at the latest? Of course, it depends on that last batch of tests they ran."

"Yes," he agreed, looking at the policeman staring at the people walking past him. The policeman assessed him with a glance and turned his attention elsewhere. "Uncle Henry looked a lot happier. I think he's getting sick and tired of schlepping back and forth to the hospital every day."

Lynn smiled at Steve, a smile that failed to reach her anxious gray eyes. She looked around quickly to be sure no one was nearby. "We need to get out of here."

"Tell me something I don't know. That was good thinking. I don't know what's going on, but this hospital is definitely not a safe place for us to be right now."

"Oh, I know what's going on," she told him. "You aren't going to believe it, but someone just tried to kill Barrett Montgomery."

Chapter Nine

The car zigged and zagged through the heavy traffic. It was child's play to follow. The distinctive red hair was easy to spot. Besides, there seemed little doubt about where he was going. The access road led only to the airport.

Finding where he'd been staying had been more difficult. Who would have expected him to be so devious?

It was disturbing that he didn't have the baby with him, but at a guess, he was meeting the person who did. He and his friend knew exactly what little Rachel was worth. Did the Rothmore girl still have her?

Damn them. Damn them all. They would not, could not, thwart all these careful plans. Soon, very soon, all that lovely money would be within easy grasp. The sound of an airplane overhead brought a tight smile.

"WHY ARE WE stopping here? We just ate."

Steve parked the car in front of the restaurant and shut off the engine. "Pay phone," he told her. "I want to call Tim again. Hopefully, he'll have some information for us."

"Go ahead. I think we'll just wait here. Rachel's being a good girl, aren't you, sweetheart?" She reached over and stroked the baby's hand. The tiny fingers closed around her index finger.

"Are you sure? You could wait inside and order a cup of coffee or something."

She looked around at the empty parking lot. "I think we'll be safe here. Besides, you'll be within my line of sight the entire time."

He gave a short nod and strode briskly to the phone. How could he look as good from the back as he did from the front? As Lynn watched him go, her mind tried to back away from the issue of Steve, but she couldn't let it alone. He had turned her nice, secure life upside down and she didn't see how she could ever right it again.

Steve had disturbed her on an unconscious level since the day they'd met. She'd always noticed him, even though she hadn't wanted to. How often had she mentally derided his life-style? And all this time, she'd been fooling herself. The more she got to know him, the more she knew he was exactly her type.

And he wanted her. But could he come to love her?

The baby made a happy sound. She gently stroked the wisps of fine hair on the child's scalp. "You know the worst part, Rachel? The more I watch him with you, the more I keep thinking about having a baby. His baby."

There. She'd said it aloud. Her gaze wandered to Steve, to find him watching her as he spoke into the telephone. She dropped her eyes quickly, afraid he might sense what she was thinking.

"You know, Rachel, I could make partner in my firm one day if I really tried, but I don't want that anymore. In fact, I don't even enjoy the challenges anymore. I'm only twenty-seven. Aren't I too young to be having a midlife crisis?"

The baby yawned and blinked up at her.

"Okay. Sorry if I'm boring you, but I'm nervous. And I'm scared. I don't know where Marcy is, Kevin is running around loose and I'm coming to depend entirely too much on Steve."

Was that a smile on the baby's face?

"Yeah, I know. He is pretty special. But you know what else, sweetheart? So are you, even if you have lousy timing and rotten sleep patterns. I always assumed I'd have a little girl like you and maybe a couple of little boys, too. Now that I've held you and cared for you, I know I want a child of my own."

The car door opened, and Lynn gave an involuntary scream.

"Hey there. Take it easy. It's only me."

Rachel began to howl and Lynn tried to cover her embarrassment by tending to the baby as Steve slid onto the seat next to her.

"You scared us," she told him.

"I'm sorry." He leaned over the seat and gentled the child with some soothing non-words. The scent of his after-shave drifted over Lynn. When he cocked his head, their lips were only inches apart. "I think I forgot to say good-morning." His mouth tenderly closed over hers.

She felt the power of his kiss in every cell of her body.

"Do you realize it's afternoon?" she said against his lips when he started to move away.

"Oh. Okay. Good afternoon."

The second kiss was even more devastating. Lynn didn't want it to ever end.

"Want to know what I learned?" he said a bit raggedly.

No, but she guessed she couldn't have what she wanted here and now.

Steve flashed that killer smile and settled back behind the steering wheel. "Barrett Montgomery is alive. He's in critical but stable condition and they've got round-the-clock police protection with him. They're taking a close look at his original accident. It happened the night Rachel appeared in our lives."

Her face blanched. "Oh, God." She sank back against the headrest.

"Tim found out that Barrett Montgomery is a British citizen. He's here on an extended work visa. Last year, he married Alice Dunne who is supposed to be an American citizen."

"Supposed to be?"

"We're having trouble tracking her down. Tim's working on both names but it will take some time to get detailed information."

"But?"

"According to Bob Haskell, Barrett and Alice haven't been living together recently."

"Oh no." She looked back at the baby in consternation.

"Haskell didn't want to create any gossip, but he's been concerned about his boss. Barrett Montgomery has been very preoccupied lately. His wife calls frequently and is always put through immediately."

"What does that mean?"

Steve shrugged. "Beats me. Haskell either didn't know or isn't saying. Maybe they're in the process of getting a divorce. Maybe Montgomery's staying away from his wife to protect her from something. I don't know, Lynn. It's just another piece of the puzzle."

"I think we've got enough pieces. What we need is some glue. What about Alice Montgomery? Have they found her yet?"

Steve shook his head. She knew he was remembering the blood in the kitchen at the Montgomery house.

"What about the man you thought you saw at the hospital? Is he a relative?"

Steve didn't respond right away. "I don't know," he said thoughtfully. "I didn't get a clear look at him. I might have been mistaken. I do know that no relative has checked in with the hospital. Tim says the police are searching for Alice. They found the mess in her kitchen, and she hasn't been back to the house yet as far as they can tell."

"Do the police know we were there?"

"If they do, they aren't saying, but that cleaning woman knows."

"At least she didn't report you." Troubled, she pinched the bridge of her nose. "If Alice is alive, she'd be looking for her baby if she could."

"You'd think so."

"You think she's dead, too, don't you?"

Steve scratched his jaw. "I don't know. Probably. I just don't know what to think about any of this."

Neither did she.

"By the way, Kevin's prints are all over your parents' place, as well as your apartment and Marcy's."

"I guess that confirms he's the slug who trashed them."

"Looks that way," he agreed.

"So what do we do now?"

"According to the MVA, based on the partial license plate number I got at the pizza place, a man by the name of Leonard Spriggs rented that car at the airport. Do you want to ride out there with me? I'd like to see if we can get some information about Mr. Spriggs."

She nodded. "Let's go."

Steve hesitated. With a tender look, he ran a knuckle down her cheek and started the car. The unexpected caress was almost her undoing. The memory of his touch on her skin stayed with her all the way to the airport.

THE NOISY TERMINAL bustled with people and activity. They wended their way to the correct counter, nearly deafened by the din of plane engines and voices yelling to be heard. The rental agent was young, pretty and not above a passing flirtation. At Steve's request, Lynn and the baby waited on a chair across from the desk. She watched the verbal exchange with admiration, and a touch of jealousy. Steve was stealing her heart, and there wasn't a thing she could do to stop it from happening.

"Come on!" Steve raced up to her. "Leonard Spriggs returned the car a short while ago. She thinks he's boarding a plane right this minute back to England."

They scurried across the concourse in time to see the British Air jet pierce the open sky.

"Damn." He thrust the baby carrier into her hand. "Wait here."

Annoyed, she gripped his arm. "This seems to be a pattern with you."

"What are you talking about?"

"Sit here. Wait there. Well, I need to use the ladies' room." She plopped the diaper bag onto an empty seat and handed Steve the carrier. "I'll be right back."

Rachel was cranky after being bounced through the airport and Lynn felt a stab of remorse as she left Steve to deal with the infant. When she returned, she spotted Steve at the ticket counter, the baby in his strong, muscled arms. Again came the thought that Rachel could be theirs. What a natural father Steve would make.

Then she spotted the diaper bag still sitting where she had set it, along with the abandoned carrier. A natural father indeed. A typical father, more than likely. It was a miracle no one had walked off with their belongings. She tucked the straps into the carrier and adjusted the blanket so it wouldn't fall out.

The feeling that she was being watched crawled up her spine without warning. She straightened and peered around. Just as in the grocery store, the sensation was eerie, but strong. The terminal was packed with people. She didn't notice anyone paying particular attention to her.

Steve was several yards away talking with a British Airways official. Just Steve's proximity calmed her. If anything happened, all she had to do was scream and he'd come running. Still, the impression of impending danger was so overpowering that she couldn't stop looking around.

Her instincts urged her to run.

It was ludicrous. Run where? Why?

Lynn couldn't fight the feeling any longer. Any movement was preferable to standing there nervously. She would go over and take the baby from Steve.

She bent to gather everything. At that moment, a large tour group, all speaking what sounded like Italian, crossed between her and the counter where he stood.

She started forward. The arm came from nowhere to clamp around her shoulder like an iron vise. A large body propelled her to one side and forward, moving her along with the group. She stumbled, but the forceful grip held her upright, even as it compelled her to walk.

"Move," a British voice snarled in her ear.

She struggled to look back and up, but the man jerked her forward. She gathered a deep breath of air, preparing to scream, when a sudden jolt in the small of her back displaced the air in a whoosh. His quiet words penetrated like a knife.

"Should you scream, I'll have to hurt you and I'll still get the babe. Continue walking."

He thought she had the baby in the carrier. Her heart tried to pound its way free of the confines of her chest. She only caught a glimpse of a hard-thrust jaw as he moved her forward.

He was leading them toward an exit. Lynn couldn't let him force her that far. Her grip on the carrier tightened. Without pausing to think, she let the diaper bag slide down her arm and crash to the floor. The man stumbled as it fell at his feet. As his grip released fractionally, she twisted away, at the same time shoving her hip into him.

The move threw him completely off-balance, but the press of people kept him from going down all the way. They also prevented her from running.

"Steve! Steve!"

Her cries barely rose above the babble. The man reached for her. She squeezed herself between a group of three women, all chattering and gesturing with wide arms. A hand clutched at her arm holding the carrier. Someone else pushed her back within his grasp. He spun her, arms grabbing for the carrier. She swung it with all her might, catching his hip.

Off-balance, she faltered, unable to steady herself. She dropped her purse and veered away as large freckled hands made another grab for her. Lynn twisted and fell, ignobly landing on her bottom. The crowd surged around her and she rolled to the side, grateful that Rachel wasn't inside the sturdy plastic as it bounced on the tile floor.

There were people everywhere. Arms reached for her. She pulled away, shouting for Steve. The crowd stopped, blocking her view. Someone attempted to help her stand. She fought free from those unknown hands and heard Rachel's loud wail.

Suddenly, Steve's voice rose over the din. Then he was there. He helped her to stand. His arm protectively encircled her. Thank God, he still had the baby.

"Are you okay? What happened?"

"He tried to take Rachel," she told him, her voice unnaturally shrill.

"Who?" Steve searched the crowd. They were hemmed in and security was descending.

"The man from the restaurant."

Steve's eyes narrowed. "It couldn't have been. Leonard Spriggs just boarded that plane we saw take off."

"No," she protested. "He was right here. He thought I had Rachel in the carrier. He was trying to force me outside."

"That's impossible. Are you sure?"

"Of course I'm sure."

Security arrived in the form of two uniformed men. "What's the problem, folks?"

Lynn instinctively leaned against Steve as the men stared at the tableau in suspicion.

"It's okay," he assured them calmly. "My wife is still shaky. She had a dizzy spell and fell." He turned to her then, his dark eyes demanding her to go along. "Are you okay now, darling?"

"Yes. I think so." Her voice was faint, which was exactly how she felt. "I just got dizzy. I'm so embarrassed." She lowered her head to protect her face. With shaky fingers, she tried to soothe the baby. "Good thing I wasn't holding Rachel."

"Why don't you sit down over here, ma'am. We'll call for a stretcher and get you checked out."

"Oh, no! Please. I'm fine." She didn't have to feign panic at the thought. "I just need to go home. Please, Steve. Can't you just take me home?"

Steve ignored the two men and lifted the baby carrier from the floor. "I told you it was too soon to come to the airport. Your mother would have made the plane just fine without you along. Sit down for a moment and rest, darling." He turned to the onlookers. "She's had a rough time of it, C-section, you know? But she insisted on seeing off her mother."

One of the security men relaxed. "I know what you mean. I've got a headstrong wife at home myself. We'll be happy to take her over to First Aid and have her checked out if you'd like."

Lynn knew a cue when she heard one. "Please, I just want to go home and lie down."

"Okay. Thanks, fellows, but you heard my wife. I'll take her home."

The smaller of the two men bent down to retrieve the diaper bag. "Is this yours?"

"Yes, thank you."

Lynn looked up then. "My purse. Where's my purse?"

A quick glance at the floor and the nearby people showed there was no sign of a purse.

"You didn't bring your purse, remember, darling? You were just carrying the diaper bag."

Lynn swallowed her fear and nodded. "Oh. I forgot. I really am sorry."

A new voice rent the air. "Steve? My God, is that really you? I hardly recognized you."

Steve pivoted to face the three people heading toward them. The man and one of the women were remarkably tall. It was the man who had called out. A shorter, dark-haired woman walked with them. She was heavily pregnant, and her eyes were wide as she took in the scene.

"Jeff, you old son of a gun," Steve greeted heartily before anyone could utter another word. "It's been, what, two years? And this must be your new wife. Hi. I'm Steve Polansky."

The tall man stopped dead on the concourse, his face a comical mixture of shock and disbelief. The shorter woman paused, her lips parted in open surprise. The other woman merely let go of Jeff's arm and stood regarding the scene in confusion.

"I don't think you've ever met my wife, have you?" Steve rushed on. "And this is our daughter. She's three weeks old today. We were just down here seeing my mother-in-law off. What are you doing here?"

The mark of a true professional, Lynn thought, somewhat dazed by it all. Jeff hardly lost a beat before coming forward to shake her hand and smiling warmly. The smile didn't hide the puzzlement that clearly showed in his eyes.

The security man laid a hand on her shoulder, diverting her attention. "Are you sure everything is okay now?" he asked kindly.

"Oh. Yes. Thank you. Thank you very much for your help."

He smiled and nodded to Steve, who added his own thanks as he fastened Rachel into the carrier. Without really seeming to, he guided their little group forward so they kept moving toward the exit that was only a few feet away. His voice was hearty and happy as he and Jeff made banal conversation.

"You must be Jerrilynn," the pregnant woman said quietly. "I'm Petey and this is Gail." Both women kept pace alongside Lynn as they progressed through the busy concourse. "Are you okay? What's going on?"

The smile was weak, but Lynn didn't even know where she got the strength for that much. "I wish I knew. The man Steve claims is inside a plane headed for England just tried to take the baby again, and while I was fighting him off, someone stole my purse."

The two women exchanged glances. Petey laid a gentle hand on Lynn's arm. "Welcome to our world."

"Someone stole your purses, too?"

"Nope. We married detectives."

A DEEP HACKING COUGH pulled her from the cavern of sleep into which she'd crawled. Her chest hurt. She couldn't breathe. Restlessly, she twisted and turned away from the heat. Then her eyes blinked in the swirling darkness and she sucked air futilely. Desperately, her lungs attempted to expel the heavy smoke-filled air.

Smoke?

The air was foul, thick with billowing clouds of dense smoke. A crackling sound drew her eyes to the far wall. Her drugged mind tried to assimilate what she saw. A sheet of orange fire aggressively marched across the wall, lapping at the ceiling even as it spread outward.

Fire!

She needed to escape. She needed air. Her chest contracted in pain as her lungs scrambled to draw oxygen from the depleted air without success. From far away came the sound of pounding. It barely registered. She twisted against the pressure on her chest. With what remained of her strength, she managed to roll from the bed, even as a tongue of yellow-orange fire snapped at the hem of the ugly green bedspread. Terror, complete and absolute, filled her mind in that instant. She was going to die.

She never heard the shattering of the windowpane. She never felt the wicked heat of the flames as they swirled forward with renewed energy at the sudden influx of air. She didn't know when they raced across the carpet for a taste of her clothing.

LYNN SETTLED BACK against the seat of the rental car and snuck dubious peeks at Steve's rugged profile. His shoulders were straight and there was a concentrated set to his features. He had barely said a word to her since they'd left the airport, but she sensed he was pensive rather than angry.

Lynn was impressed by Steve's friends. They were unconditionally supportive. Apparently, on the way to the parking lot, Steve managed to fill Jeff in with a rough outline of events. Petey had offered Lynn the use of her credit card, while Jeff's wife, Gail, had asked how she could help.

Lynn considered the people she normally associated with on a daily basis. There were people she called friends and saw socially, but she wondered if even one of them would be as generous toward her as these two women she knew only by name. They accepted her and were ready to do whatever it took to help because of Steve. Only a special kind of man could command that type of loyalty—and only special friends would supply it.

Jeff rented a car for them in his name, but it came without a telephone. Once they were off the highway, Steve found a public phone and pulled over, leaving Lynn and Rachel in the car.

"You still running free?" Tim asked.

"Shouldn't I be?" Steve responded cautiously.

A sigh filled his ear. "There's a pickup order out on you. Someone connected you to the bearded man."

"I shaved."

Tim's hearty laugh filled his ear. "Good thinking. I believe we've found our reason for the kidnapping. If the baby belongs to Barrett Montgomery, the baby is an heir. There's big money involved. Barrett Montgomery's father is none other than Edgar Armitage Montgomery, Lord Harley."

"Say what?"

"It's the way the British do their titles. Just call him Edgar for short. Seriously, he's a wealthy British industrialist with connections that once led back to the

Crown. He was a very powerful and influential man, with a direct ear to some important decision makers in England."

Steve rubbed his chin absently and stared at the empty wall in front of him. "Was?"

"He suffered a series of strokes. The family was told to expect him to die over a year ago, but his body simply refused to give up, even though his mind has been gone for a long time now."

"So the family is just waiting for him to die so they can inherit?"

"Not exactly. Barrett, his baby brother, Herbert, and their sister, Guenevere, are all stamped from their father's mold," Tim continued. "They've all made private fortunes of their own, but until recently, only Herbert was married. His wife is expecting their first child, as a matter of fact. Unfortunately, neither Herbert nor his offspring inherit the title. That honor goes to Barrett. I don't imagine Lord Harley would have been thrilled by his eldest's sudden marriage to an American nobody, or the way Barrett set about producing an heir right away."

"Thus making baby Rachel very important in the scheme of Lord Harley's life," Steve said.

He could almost see Tim nod. "That's my thought. Someone figures they can hold her hostage for a lot of money."

"Then why kill Barrett?"

Tim sighed. "I have no idea. He's holding his own, by the way. The police are quietly searching for Alice Montgomery, and they haven't yet connected you to her disappearance."

Steve stopped moving his fingers when he realized they were beating out a staccato rhythm on the shelf of the telephone stand.

"I told our inquisitive friends that you were taking a well-earned vacation after our last case."

Steve could just imagine how the police bought into that. Particularly when they learned Lynn was his next-door neighbor.

"You probably won't be surprised to hear that Kevin Goldlund has a record," Tim went on. "Petty theft and one charge of grand larceny. The charges were dropped on the big one and he was a juvenile for the petty theft, but recently, the police were starting to look at him again."

"For what?"

"They aren't saying."

"You think he went big-time with the kidnapping?"

Tim made a rude noise. "Not by himself, he didn't. But you'll be interested to know he started work a short time ago for a lawn service."

"Why am I interested in that?"

"One of his accounts was the Montgomery place on River Road."

Steve chewed back an expletive. It was almost too neat. Something didn't compute, but before he could finish the thought, Tim continued speaking.

"On a different subject, do you know an Alan Burkley?"

Steve's mind switched tracks and sprang to attention. The real estate agent must have news on the offer Steve had made for the land that would supply his dream. "Yeah, I know him."

"He's been trying to get hold of you. He wants you to call him right away or after eight tonight." Tim paused as though waiting for an explanation, but he waited in vain.

"Thanks, Tim. Did he give you a number?"

"Yeah."

When Tim hung up, Steve dialed the number for Alan Burkley. The real estate agent was so pleased, he was effervescent. Steve's offer had been accepted. The news was almost too good to believe. His long-term goal was just about in his grasp and the thought scared him. Steve knew what usually happened when he wanted something this badly.

He hung up and returned to the car deep in thought. Lynn took one look at his face and remained silent as he put the vehicle in gear. It wasn't until they were stuck in the infamous D.C. traffic that he came out of his reverie and repeated what he had learned from Tim.

Lynn stared at Steve's profile and thought again how good-looking he was without the beard. "I wish I knew what compelled Marcy to bring the baby to me. It would answer so much."

"Yeah. If she knew the baby was kidnapped, why didn't she go to the police?" He frowned as a fire truck lumbered its awkward way past the bottleneck and continued up the street. Ahead of them, dense smoke darkened the crystal sky.

"Why are we assuming the baby was kidnapped? We don't know that." Lynn watched his strong fingers tighten on the steering wheel then relax.

"You're right, but it fits so nicely."

"Square pegs and round holes, buster. You can use a hammer, but you can't make it fit. Kevin didn't have anything to do with this baby."

Traffic came to a stop again and Steve frowned at her. "Why do you say that?"

"After he forced me into the car, he asked me whose baby it was. Steve, he didn't have a clue. He wasn't faking. If he'd wanted Rachel, he would have taken her instead of me."

"You didn't mention this before."

His penetrating gaze returned to the street as they surged forward another few feet.

"I forgot. But since he didn't know who the baby belonged to, he couldn't have given her to Marcy."

Steve rubbed his jaw and met her bewildered look. "Then we're back where we started."

"Not quite. We know who Rachel is. But why is Kevin tearing up our apartments?"

Steve snapped his fingers and shot her a triumphant grin as the traffic began to inch forward yet again. "The drugs. You said all along the bag didn't belong to Marcy."

"Of course." Excited, she looked around without really seeing any of her surroundings, relieved at Steve's assessment. "I knew they didn't belong to her. She must have taken them from Kevin. She probably saw my missing jewelry and decided to return it."

"Okay," he agreed. "I'll buy that. Kevin tears up Marcy's place in frustration and then goes to your place."

"It's the next logical place for Marcy to go. After that, he goes to my parents' house."

The police had figured a way to reroute the cars around the source of the fire. Steve pulled forward half a car length before turning for a quick view of his companion. Her face was alive with animation.

"And we show up and interrupt his search," he concluded. "But why is Marcy's car there? Where is she? And who is the man who was shooting at you? Damn! I forgot to check out that red car."

"Maybe Marcy was hiding someplace inside the house."

Steve remembered feeling that he wasn't alone in the house. It was possible. Marcy could have been in the cellar or a closet. He hadn't exactly checked everything in a thorough manner.

"Okay, maybe. But where does the idiot with the gun come in?"

"He was chasing Kevin, not me."

Steve frowned. "His supplier, maybe? That would make sense, too. If Marcy took Kevin's drugs and his supplier or a customer wanted them, it would explain why Kevin was so frantic."

"This is all well and good," she said, "but what does any of it have to do with Rachel?"

"If we're right, nothing at all. Kevin becomes a side issue."

"Then why did Marcy give you the baby?"

There was no answer to that question.

Their attention was drawn to the host of fire trucks, ambulances and police cars that blocked most of the road. By now, the smell of smoke was discernible. They were finally close enough to the source of the commotion to see that the building on fire was a rundown motel unit. Then they turned off Wisconsin onto a side road on a detour around the sight.

"It's hopeless." Lynn sighed.

"No, it's not. There's an explanation. We just don't have enough information yet to figure out what it is. If only we could find your sister."

She slanted him a look. "We haven't tried my brother's place yet. Marcy may have gone there."

"I guess it's worth a shot. Give me some directions."

They weren't far away from her brother's apartment complex in Bethesda.

Steve saw the flashing lights even as they rounded the corner of her brother's street. Lots of flashing lights. All of them sitting in front of a small apartment building. He didn't have to be told whose building. He knew. The local police were having a busy day.

"Slow down. What are you doing? That's my brother's place up ahead."

"I know. The one with half the police force in front of it. We can't stop, Lynn."

"But Marcy might be in there."

"And she might not. I'm going to park two streets over and walk back. The police might know your face, but they won't know mine. If she's there, I'll find out."

Steve drove past as quickly as the narrow lane for cars would allow. There was very little room for traffic with all the parked cars and ambulance out front. A crowd of onlookers had gathered, but what snared Steve's attention was the yellow police line that had gone up. And then something else riveted his gaze. Two attendants were loading a body bag into the coroner's van.

Chapter Ten

"What do you mean, there's been an accident?"

The red-haired man paced the room as far as the telephone cord would allow. He felt sick. Quite likely, he had a fever. The wound in his side was festering.

"Bloody hell... Of course I'll deal with it... Don't I always handle things?" He stopped pacing to listen to the voice on the other end. His curse was low and heartfelt. He perched on the side of the bed and grimaced. Why was everything going so bloody wrong?

"I'll see to it... Righto... No... That's not necessary. There's nothing you could do by coming over here now... Yes. Of course I'll ring you... Yes, immediately."

He replaced the receiver and stared blankly at a wall, trying to decide a proper course of action. Lenny would have come in a bit handy at the moment. Well, there was no point in regrets. He'd simply have to see to this business himself. The babe would have to wait. But if he got his hands on that bloody woman again, this time he really would kill her.

STEVE PARKED around the corner. "Wait here and I'll find out what I can."

"Not a chance." Lynn was already stepping from the car. "That's my brother's apartment."

"All the more reason for you to wait here. Someone might recognize you."

"You said I was beyond recognition."

"Lynn, they're looking for a man and a woman with a baby."

"Fine. You take the baby. There are hundreds of couples with babies, Steve," she told him, mimicking his earlier words to her. "You won't stand out. You don't even have a beard."

His protest died before it was uttered. She marched away, hips swaying in a tantalizing rhythm. His lips split in a self-mocking grin. Darn, but she was a gutsy lady. A man would never get bored around Lynn. And she sure did wonders for that pair of jeans he had bought her. He undid the carrier and followed her up the street. He had to work to keep the smile off his face.

"Well, kid," he told the baby, "it's you and me this time. We'll see if we can get our own information."

He didn't glance in Lynn's direction when he joined the throng of curious onlookers, but he was aware of her and where she was every second. It wasn't hard to insinuate himself into one of the knots of people clustered about. It was harder to work his way forward so he could stand near a group that might have been here long enough to have really seen something useful. Steve selected a teenage boy to approach. He was standing to one side near the roped-off area with two other, younger boys. Excitement fairly danced from the three of them.

"What's going on?" he asked.

The boys examined him, but apparently saw nothing to worry them. Steve kept his expression curious and openly friendly. "We could see the commotion from upstairs," he added with a gesture in the direction of the building. That was enough to establish him as a possible neighbor to the group. The older boy nodded at the police line in front of the building.

"Some guys broke in and started trashing my neighbor's apartment. The cops think they were looking for drugs or money. Only they got in a fight and one of them pulled a gun." His chest pushed forward importantly. "I heard the first shot because we're on the second floor where they broke in. There's a bullet hole in the wall right by the elevator. I saw it." Unsuppressed excitement filled his voice.

"Yeah? Well I saw the dude come flying out the front door," interjected one of the younger boys. "Me and Mom were just gettin' outta the car to go see Uncle Jim when this guy pointed the gun and blam, blam, blam! You shoulda seen it."

Steve frowned at the bloodthirsty youth, but he read past the bravado to the shaky emotions underneath. He slanted a look at the others. He understood that the teens had to appear brave and unconcerned or lose face. None of them was likely to forget seeing their first dead body any time soon.

"What happened to the guy with the gun?" Steve asked quietly.

"The guy in 212 is an off-duty cop. He saw the whole thing," the older boy explained. "He lives right across the hall, ya know? You've probably seen his patrol car in the parking lot. Anyhow, he jumped off his balcony and chased after the dude with the gun."

Steve looked at the balconies and was impressed. Even if the cop lived right above the garden apartments, it was still a pretty good distance to jump.

"Yeah," the youngest boy agreed. "He tackled him just like on television. My mom wouldn't let me see any more," he stated in a disgusted voice. "But they caught him. I saw 'em put him in the back of a police car a little while ago."

"And they were both men, huh?" Steve asked.

"Yep. Not even kids. Old guys. Maybe in their thirties. I heard Mom tell the cops that."

Steve bit back a comment on the "old guys" reference and nodded encouragingly, but just then, a woman called to the youngest boy in a tone of voice that had him scurrying away.

Lynn caught his eye and separated herself from the throng. She ambled carelessly down the sidewalk along with several other people. The excitement was drawing to a close.

Steve followed at a more leisurely pace and found Lynn waiting inside the car. With troubled eyes, she watched as he secured the baby. They didn't speak until Steve had the car in gear and was pulling out into traffic.

"Kevin's dead."

"What? How can you possibly know that?"

"I was talking to a little old lady who saw the whole thing. She was pretty shook up."

But not so shaken up she couldn't tell the gory details to anyone who would listen, Steve thought. Wisely, he refrained from stating that aloud. "How do you know it was Kevin?"

"How many men in green windbreakers have been going around shooting at people in the past twenty-four hours? Besides, she gave me a pretty good description of both men. Kevin must have broken into my brother's place and the other man followed him."

"Lynn." He laid a hand on her arm. "You're speculating, honey."

"Speculating nothing. I saw him. Didn't you? The gunman was sitting in the back seat of the police cruiser when we drove past the first time. I got a good look at him as we went by. I didn't know about Kevin then, of course, but you don't forget a man who points a gun at you. It was the same man who was at my parents' house."

Steve uttered an expletive. He hadn't seen the figure in the police car. He'd been staring at the body bag.

"And you think the dead man is Kevin?"

"Who else? The description sure fits, right down to the scratches on Kevin's face. Also, my brother lives on the second floor."

That seemed to sum it up all nice and tidy. And if Kevin was dead, they really needed to get rid of the drugs in the bottom of the diaper bag. Steve decided to flush them down the toilet as soon as they got back to the hotel.

"I'm really worried about Marcy now, Steve. She could be in real danger. I wonder where she is."

So did he. Steve rested a hand on Lynn's thigh. The unexpected contact startled both of them. He felt her muscles stiffen, saw the rosy blush sweep her skin and heard her sudden intake of breath.

Rachel started to cry.

"We have got to find that baby's mother," he told her grimly. He started the car, looking for a telephone, to call Tim.

SETTING THE FIRE had been a nice touch. Two down and two to go. Jerrilynn Rothmore's wallet fell back to the bottom of the purse as restless fingers drummed against the steering wheel. The distinctive key card sat like a neon banner amid the cosmetics and miscellaneous junk in the purse. Lovely. Perfectly lovely. Even better was the business card stamped with the name and address of the hotel. Someone had oh so helpfully written the room number on the back. How very convenient.

Tonight would be soon enough to deal with the other Rothmore woman and the baby. Too bad there wasn't time to find out what her plan had been, but it didn't matter. There was still one other person to remove from the scene.

"To the victor go the spoils, and I intend to be the only victor. Soon that lovely money will be all mine."

"WHAT ARE we doing here?"

The Montgomery house sat against the waning daylight, deserted, yet somehow vigilant as they pulled into the driveway. There were no signs of life.

"I want another quick look at that car in the garage."

"Are you crazy?"

His dimples flashed. "I'm beginning to think so. Wait here."

"Not a chance."

His warm, hard hand stayed her movement when she would have opened the car door. "I think I know where Alice Montgomery is."

"What? Where?"

He frowned, his eyes dark with concern as he looked at her. "Spriggs couldn't have moved the body very far in the daylight."

The sheer horror of what he was implying sent her pulse hammering through her veins. "You think he put her in the car?" Visions of a body crammed into the trunk of the car made her shudder.

"It's been days, Lynn. If I'm right, you don't want to be with me when I open that trunk. Hell, I don't want to be with me."

She grabbed his wrist, feeling the throb of his pulse. "Don't go in there. We can call the police—anonymously."

"No, they might not release the information right away and we need to be sure."

Lynn shuddered and gripped him a bit tighter. "You'll hurry?"

He cupped her head and drew her close to him for a quick, unsatisfying kiss. "Count on it."

He slipped from the car almost silently. He hadn't even closed his door completely, she realized. She shivered, but not because of the temperature. Rachel whimpered, but she didn't turn to give the baby a glance. Her eyes were focused on Steve who had hurried to the door of the garage and was bent over the lock.

Silently, she urged him to hurry. She wanted to get away from here. The dark house seemed to be watching them with an air of expectancy.

The garage door swung open abruptly, but Steve paused in the act of stepping inside. He reached out and pulled the door closed, then he sprinted back to the car.

"What's wrong?" she asked.

He stuck his head inside the door. "It's gone."

"The car?" She tried to read his peculiar expression and failed. "What does that mean?"

"It means I have to go back inside the house."

"No! Steve—"

"Wait for me."

"But—"

She was talking to empty air. She watched his long legs eat up the distance between the garage and house, where he disappeared from sight. Great. What was she supposed to do now? Sooner or later, someone would notice their car sitting here. Probably sooner. What was she supposed to tell the police when they came rapping on the car door? Darn that sexy know-it-all man.

Lynn whiled away some of the time by getting into the back of the car and changing the fussy baby. Better to look natural than to cower on the front seat.

"Listen, Rachel, we need to have a talk. About last night—your timing was awful." A serious understatement. If it hadn't been for the baby, she and Steve would have been lovers by now. Her breath caught in her throat at the thought.

"What do you say we make a deal for tonight?"

STEVE WONDERED if the police had activated the security system. He decided the odds were fifty-fifty, but ninety-nine percent that they were keeping a close eye on the place. Either way, he needed to get in and get out, or he wouldn't have to worry about whether Leonard Spriggs and company had moved the car or if the police had impounded the vehicle.

They might not have turned on the alarm system, but they had relocked the doors and windows. He decided he didn't have time to finesse any of the locks. He selected the window outside the den and, wrapping his hand in his sweater, punched a hole through the glass.

No alarm screamed in protest. No police or neighbors arrived with drawn guns. In minutes, he had the window open and was over the sill and inside.

The musty, rotting smell was worse than he remembered, but he had no intention of heading for the kitchen where the stench would probably be overpowering. He flipped on the light over the desk and started going through drawers.

It was amazing what a person could collect. Especially a wealthy woman who apparently liked to shop. More revealing was what was missing. The lack of address book didn't surprise him—the police might have that, or else it was out in the kitchen. He considered that room off-limits.

"Odd." There were no personal letters or notes. No income tax information. No pay stubs or passports. "Bills, receipts and notes from the interior decorator? Where's the personal stuff? And why is everything dated within the past seven months?"

Scowling, Steve moved into the bedroom. He needed time to do a professional toss of this place. Time he didn't have. Besides, the police would have found anything obvious—and at any moment, those same police were apt to drive by to be sure everything was okay. When they saw the car sitting in the driveway...

In the bedroom closet, he got a break in the pocket of a pair of men's suit pants. Clearly, the receipt had been balled in anger more than once before it was shoved into the pocket and forgotten somewhere along the line. The receipt had gotten wet, too, at some point, making the details hard to read. It appeared to be a doctor's bill made out to Mary A. Dunne.

Mary Alice Dunne? Or maybe a relative?

Now was not the time for a contemplative study. Now was the time to get the heck out of here before some persuasive men in blue suits arrived with guns and handcuffs.

Lynn was pouring formula into a bottle when Steve came sprinting back in her direction. Instantly alarmed, she didn't wait for directions. She rebelted the baby in the carrier and got back in the passenger seat.

"What happened?" she demanded as Steve started the car and backed down the driveway. Rachel protested the delay, but they ignored her for the moment.

"Nothing, yet. I want to get out of here before we have company." He pulled out onto River Road.

She studied his strong profile as the baby continued to cry. "Did you get inside?"

"Yeah, for all the good it did."

His eyes kept flicking to the rearview mirror. Lynn found herself watching in her side mirror, as well, and wondering what she was watching for. "You didn't find anything?"

"Just a doctor's bill for a Mary A. Dunne."

"Who's she?"

Steve shrugged, turned onto the beltway and eased into traffic. "Beats the heck out of me."

"Great. You've scared me half to death over a doctor's bill for someone we don't even know."

Steve flashed her a wide grin, his dimple giving his features a young, carefree look that didn't quite reach his serious eyes. "According to Rachel's birth certificate, Alice's maiden name is Dunne. Tim can't seem to find any record of her. I'm hoping this will help us locate her family."

"Oh. How's that going to help?"

"Well, for one thing, we're going to feel pretty stupid if she's off somewhere visiting family and the blood in the kitchen belongs to the cook or the cleaning woman or something."

"Three weeks after having a baby? And not taking the baby with her? I don't think so."

"Neither do I, Lynn. But look at it this way, we've been assuming, primarily because of Lenny's accent, that Barrett Montgomery was the intended victim. What if the truth is related to something in Alice's background?"

"But they tried to kill Barrett in intensive care."

"Uh-huh. Maybe someone wants both of them dead." He pulled off the highway and headed toward the hotel.

Lynn was thankful when they stopped so she could stick a bottle in Rachel's mouth and stop the waterworks. So was Rachel.

They trudged inside and up to the suite. Lynn collapsed on the couch with the baby in her arms, feeling bone-weary. Steve flipped on the television set on his way to the bathroom. Lynn paid scant attention until the screen filled with fire trucks and smoke. It was the motel fire they had passed.

"Steve!"

"Right here." He turned up the volume and they watched a stretcher being loaded into an ambulance.

"...Giselle Rothmore was taken to Shady Grove Adventist Hospital where she is listed in stable condition."

"That's my mother's name!"

"She is suffering from minor burns, smoke inhalation and a drug overdose," the commentator continued. "At this time, it is not clear how the fire ori—"

"My mother? It can't be my mother! She's in Aus...Marcy!"

They said the name together and returned their gazes to the screen, but already the commentator was moving on.

"Did he say drug overdose?"

Steve's caring eyes filled with sympathy. "And arson."

"Arson?" The word was a whisper in the room, lost in Rachel's frantic cries. Only then did Lynn realize she had withdrawn the food from the hungry infant.

SHADY GROVE WAS the same hospital Barrett Montgomery was in. That wasn't altogether surprising since it was also the closest one to the fire scene. Steve tried to make time in the heavy traffic.

"You do realize," he said softly, "the police will be there. They'll want to talk to us."

"Me, not us. I'm going in alone."

His head whipped in her direction. "The hell you are."

"The hell I'm not. This time, you'll have to wait in the car with the baby."

"Lynn—"

"She's my sister." And that basically said it all. "Besides, we can't take the baby inside, you know that."

"Lynn—"

She ignored the husky sound of her name on his lips. "You need to be free to figure out what's going on. I don't plan to tell the police a single thing."

"Lynn—"

"I plan to stand on my constitutional right not to incriminate myself." But she wished fervently that Rachel hadn't interrupted things between them last night. "Do you know any good attorneys?"

He saw from the firm tilt to her chin that she meant every word. She'd do it, too. She'd sit there without saying a word for as long as it took. Lynn would march into hell for someone she cared about, and she'd added him to her list. His throat jammed with emotion.

"I have an idea," he said quietly.

LYNN DIDN'T ASK where he got the nurse's uniform when he hurried into the parking lot. He was bold enough and determined enough to have taken it off some poor woman. Lynn had never had a champion before. It felt strange yet wonderful. It felt like love.

Steve pulled other things from the brown paper sack, as well. There was a name tag, and all the accoutrements to go with the uniform, including hosiery two sizes larger than she wore.

Steve shrugged. "I just took everything inside the locker. The sweater should cover the fact that the clothes are too big. You can stick something in the toes of the shoes. Besides, they tie."

His hand sought hers.

"Are you sure you're okay with this?" he questioned.

She gripped his fingers fiercely.

"I promise, I'll keep your name out. I'll—"

"Hush." He lifted her hand to his mouth and brushed his lips over her knuckles. "If you get caught, you tell them the truth."

"But—"

His smile was soft, etching a new niche in her heart. "Remember when I told you I had other dreams and plans?"

Her breath caught in her throat. "Yes?"

"I bought an airpark last night."

"What?"

He smiled with his whole face this time. "It's been a dream of mine for a long time. I worked at a small airstrip when I was in high school and served some time in the air force. When I left, I knew I wanted to own my own small airport—to teach flying and maybe parachuting. You'd better get dressed."

Her hands automatically moved to the waistband of her jeans. "Parachuting? Are you crazy?"

The smile became a naughty grin. "Well, flying, anyhow."

"But aren't there regulations?" She struggled out of the jeans and into the white stockings, thankful they were parked in the empty far corner of the lot. "I mean, you can't just buy a strip of land and make it an airport."

"That's right. In fact, you can't establish a new airpark anywhere in this county. That's why I had to find an existing one. Fortunately for me, there is such a place. It hasn't been used in over twenty years, but the original owner kept the license valid and he was willing to sell it since he's moved away. He no longer owns the property, simply the license. The property came up for sale a few months ago, and the real estate agent called to tell me they've accepted my bid."

How had she once thought this man lacked ambition?

She scooched way down, pulled the sweatshirt and T-shirt over her head in one fast motion and slid the white dress down in its place, conscious of Steve watching intently. "Doesn't that take money? Big money."

He shrugged, but there was a heated look to his eyes as he watched her struggling with buttons. "Not really. Both the land and the license went pretty cheaply, and I've been saving every penny since almost forever."

"That explains your apartment."

His grin was teasing. "Don't like my novel taste in decorating, huh? Anyhow, I have enough capital to get my business started, but it means I'll be skirting debt for a lot of years. On the plus side, there's a house on the land as well as a couple of hangars and some other outbuildings. I already own two small planes. It's enough to get me going."

The shoes were too big, but Steve was right, the laces should help keep them on her feet long enough to get her past a police guard.

Steve started the engine. "I'll drive up to the front door and drop you off. It will look more natural and you won't have so far to walk."

"Oh, but—"

He pulled in front of the main entrance and reached over to capture her hand. "Your sister will be okay."

"Thanks." She intended to press a light kiss on his lips, but Steve had other ideas. He kissed her hard and deep as if he never wanted to let her go. She was still quivering all over when she entered the hospital.

The elderly woman at the information desk sent her to the fourth floor. If she was surprised by Lynn's request, she didn't show it. Feeling like an obvious fraud, Lynn squared her shoulders and tried to act as if she belonged there. Amazingly, no one gave her a second glance.

Marcy's room was easy enough to spot. It was the one with a uniformed officer sitting outside. She swallowed hard, took a deep breath and stepped forward briskly. The smile she gave the officer's upturned face was stiff and oh so brittle. He nodded and she was inside, just that easy.

Marcy lay very still in the far bed on the right. They had tied her in some kind of restraints. Oxygen and other tubes sprouted from her, making her look like some haywire experiment. Lynn felt sick.

Her sister's dark hair sharply contrasted with the white sheets, so close in color to her pale features. Someone had cleaned her up, but the subtle scent of smoke lingered past the smell of antiseptic. She opened groggy eyes when Lynn called her name and touched her shoulder.

"Sorry," Marcy whispered. Her words were slurred and difficult to hear. "Knew you'd be mad. They make me feel so alive."

Did she mean the drugs?

"Don't talk, Marce. It's okay. Everything will be okay now." Tears filled Lynn's eyes and she wiped angrily at the moisture. "Just rest."

"No. Have to tell you. They knocked her against the counter and she didn't move. I was afraid of the police. The drugs..." The rest of the words were indecipherable, lost in a fit of coughing.

"It's okay, Marcy. Don't try to talk."

"Scary. There was blood. I was supposed to babysit. Kevin worked for her. He was stealing. I'm sorry, Lynn."

She closed her eyes and coughed some more. Lynn wiped at more tears, even as she stroked her sister's wan cheek.

"I reco'nized Lenny," Marcy's hoarse, whispery voice went on, growing more faint and groggy with each word. "Kevin met him in a bar, but they weren't frien's. He wouldn' buy any pills. They made me feel so good." Her eyes opened in a plea for understanding, and then closed as another bout of coughing racked her chest.

Lynn turned her ravaged face to the window, wishing for the comfort of Steve's arms.

STEVE FOUND a parking space close to the front door and debated his next course of action. Drugs. They still had all those drugs in the bottom of the diaper bag.

His heart nearly pounded through his chest. How could he have been so stupid? If the police caught Lynn now or found him sitting out here in plain sight with the pills in the bag... He didn't want to consider the consequences.

He couldn't just abandon Rachel to run inside and find a rest room. And he couldn't see taking her into the men's room. Damn it, how did single fathers manage with daughters?

He looked around. There wasn't even a trash can in sight. No way was he just going to dump these drugs on the ground, so what was the alternative?

Steve grabbed the diaper bag and the baby carrier and hurried into the building. On the second floor, he found what he was looking for. An unoccupied room. Rachel cooed up at him as he set the carrier and the diaper bag on the bed. He shut the door to the hall, belatedly discovering that it had no lock, and stepped inside the bathroom.

He opened all four containers and emptied them over the toilet. The pills collected obscenely in the bottom of the bowl. The water flushed, the pills didn't. Someone knocked on the door.

"Just a minute."

The response wasn't in English. Steve wiped at a bead of sweat and held the door handle to prevent entry. Whoever it was went away. With a quick glance to be sure Rachel was okay, he went back into the bathroom and tried again. It took three tries to flush the pills from sight. By then, he was sweating profusely.

He wiped his forehead and looked around. There was no place to hide the empty containers. Leaving them here would only point fingers if the wrong people found them. Quickly, he rinsed them out and wiped away all traces of his fingerprints. Then he stuffed them into his pocket. There were bins for trash in the lobby. At least now if they were searched, both he and Lynn could deny any knowledge of their former contents. There would be no way to prove otherwise.

He heard Rachel, even as he stepped from the bathroom. The main door flung open to reveal a forbidding woman in white. She reminded him of a lieutenant colonel he'd once known. The lieutenant colonel hadn't liked his dimples. Hopefully, the nurse didn't share the man's bias.

"What are you doing in here?" she demanded.

With an apologetic, and he hoped, embarrassed, smile, he motioned toward the baby. "I'm sorry. I didn't mean to cause any problems. I just didn't want to drag my daughter into a men's room and this room was empty, so..." He gave a self-deprecating shrug.

The harridan's face softened a trifle. "These rooms are for patients' use only. You should have asked someone to hold her for you." Rachel cooed, winning another admirer. "How old is she?"

A few minutes later, he was back downstairs in the main lobby. He settled in a chair with the baby next to him, pitched the pill containers in a tall gray bin, and wondered how Lynn was doing. For her sake, he hoped Marcy would be okay.

While Rachel was occupied staring around at the busy lobby, he fished for the paper he had found in the Montgomery house. The bill was dated almost two years ago. The ink was faded and even missing in places, but he could read the doctor's name and the name of the clinic. The Sunrise Clinic, Dr. Matthew Abrams. The initials after the name were indecipherable, as was the address, but he could make out most of the phone number.

Steve dug out his calling card, lifted the baby seat and headed for the bank of pay phones. With Rachel in the carrier at his feet, he looked in the telephone book under zip codes to find out where the area code originated. The Orlando area of Florida. Interesting. He thought about the picture of the young couple on the beach. If Alice Dunne was from Florida, maybe that was why Tim was having trouble running her down.

The first number he tried rang busy, so he made another guess and got an elderly woman with a hearing problem. He went back to the first try and the line was still busy. His next guess was a pizza parlor. He curbed an impulse to ask them if they delivered. The first line was clear now, but rang unanswered. He was about to give up when a cheerful feminine voice answered, "Sunrise Clinic."

"Dr. Matthew Abrams, please."

"I'm sorry, sir. Dr. Abrams is out of the building until Monday."

"Oh. Well, I'm trying to get some information on a former patient."

The voice chilled to subzero. "I'm sorry, sir. We don't give out patient information."

"No, no, I'm not asking for confidential information. I'm trying to locate someone who is missing."

"You'll have to call Dr. Abrams on Monday morning."

"Wait! Don't hang up. Can you tell me what sort of a clinic Sunrise is? I mean, is it a women's center, a general—"

"Sunrise Clinic covers all manner of treatment from simple depression to clinical psychoses. You'll need to call back on Monday if you want specific information. Our marketing people are not here on weekends."

"Okay. Thanks..." He was talking to dead air. Now what the hell did that mean? And who was Mary Dunne?

Chapter Eleven

He couldn't still be alive. It was intolerable. The man must die. He would die! The baby was worthless as long as he lived. The car crash hadn't killed him, and the knife wound hadn't killed him, so what would? He wasn't a superhero, and even cats only had nine lives.

"Bastard. Stinking bastard."

A hand, trembling with fury, wiped away the spittle and repeatedly pounded the steering wheel. "He should be dead. Why isn't he dead?"

It wasn't fair.

It was unendurable.

"No more mistakes. Whatever it takes, whatever it costs. This time, damn him, he dies."

STEVE SAW LYNN step off the elevator. She looked exhausted. It was plain in the slight slump of her shoulders and the weary way she pushed away a strand of hair as she paused to survey the lobby. When she spotted him, her expression brightened, warming him clear through. She lifted her chin and her lips turned up at the corners. She might be going through hell, but she was smart and gutsy and beautiful in all the ways that counted. She started briskly in his direction.

He gave her a quick hug. "You okay?"

"Fine."

"Marcy?"

Her eyes clouded.

"Come on," he said. "Let's go to the cafeteria and get something to eat."

Settled at a back table, Lynn haltingly told him what Marcy had said. "She wasn't very coherent, Steve. And I didn't dare stay too long and make the guard suspicious."

"You did great. At least now, we can piece together most of it." He watched her take a sip of coffee and noticed the fine flutter of her delicate hand. He wished they were someplace private so he could give in to the urge to hold her.

"Marcy saw them kill Alice Montgomery and couldn't go to the police because of the drugs," Lynn told him. "Apparently, Kevin worked for the Montgomerys. Lenny struck up an acquaintance with him at some bar."

"Probably to pump him for inside information about the Montgomery household."

"That's what I figured. Lenny must be Leonard Spriggs, but there were two men. Marcy referred to *them,* not *him.*"

"So Spriggs had an accomplice."

"I guess so, but who?"

"First rule of detecting, sweetheart. Always follow the money. Let's assume this whole plot was a kidnap attempt. Rachel is worth a lot of money to her grandfather, but also, I would think, to her parents."

"Then why kill Alice?"

"It could have been a mistake."

"Yes, but someone tried to kill Barrett Montgomery, too."

"Who stands to gain if Rachel's parents are suddenly removed from the picture?"

"Another relative?"

He tapped the tip of her nose and watched her lovely gray eyes widen. "Bingo. Barrett's brother, Herbert, is next in line for Daddy's money and his title. He would also have a British accent." Steve felt sure this was the answer. "Barrett wasn't living apart from his wife and daughter because of an impending divorce, he was trying to protect them from brother Herbert."

"You think so?"

"It makes sense." Steve fished for a quarter. "I'm going to give Tim a call and see if he can find out if Herbert Montgomery is here in the States or still in England. Will you be okay here for a few minutes?"

Her tired eyes smiled at him. "We'll be fine. I'll just finish this cardboard sandwich."

"Thatta girl. I'll hurry."

He dropped a kiss on the top of her head, afraid to get near those potent lips, and headed to the pay phones he could see across the way.

"Timing is everything," Tim said in response to Steve's greeting. "I just found out Barrett's brother has been in the States since last week—along with a friend of his."

"Leonard Spriggs."

"Leonard Spriggs," Tim confirmed.

"And does Herbert have a cash-flow problem?"

"That will take more time," Tim told him. "On paper, Herbert has a thriving business."

Steve had to shift in order to see Lynn and the baby through the glass window of the cafeteria. Her warm brown hair fell around her face as she bent to talk to Rachel.

"Hey, you still there?" Tim asked.

"Yeah. Sorry. What were you saying?"

"I said I still don't have anything on Alice Dunne."

Steve watched Lynn lift the baby from the car seat and cuddle her. She would make a good mother.

"It's probably moot at this point since Marcy saw Lenny and Herbert kill Alice, but I've got the name of a psychiatric clinic near Orlando with a bill made out to Mary A. Dunne. Probably her mother or some other relative. The clinic isn't very receptive to questions."

"Whoa. Back up. Marcy saw a murder?"

"That's what she told Lynn."

Tim uttered an expletive.

"Yeah. That about sums it up. It must have happened in the kitchen, which means I messed up evidence at a crime scene. The cops are going to love me."

"Damn. Did you talk to the sister?"

"No, Lynn snuck in dressed as a nurse." He watched her playing with Rachel. Would a little girl of hers have that same saucy brown hair?

Tim made another rude noise. "Your Lynn sounds special."

"Yeah."

Tim paused as though surprised. "Er, any idea what they did with Alice's body?" he asked quietly.

"I think so. A light blue sedan disappeared from the Montgomery garage. I never checked it the first time I was there. It's probably on the bottom of the Potomac right now."

"I hate to say this, but you need to talk to the cops right away," Tim said.

"I know."

"What did you do with the items from the car?"

Steve knew immediately which items he meant. Mindful of the man who had lifted the receiver next to him, he couched his answer carefully. "The contents went down the drain. I tossed the containers. The wearable items are a little tricky. Only a couple of them belong to Lynn. I don't know what to do with the rest until we talk to Marcy."

Both men were silent. Steve thought about the stolen jewelry while watching Lynn pull a bottle from the diaper bag. Rachel was getting ready to do one of her favorite things—eat.

"Why don't you put the others in an envelope and mail it back to the office?" Tim suggested. "Address it to me and mark it Personal. If we can't determine ownership, we'll send them to the boys in blue anonymously."

"Good idea."

"What are you going to do about the baby?"

Steve thought about Rachel's tiny face and sighed. "Since Barrett Montgomery is still alive, I guess adoption is out of the question."

LYNN TOOK Rachel into a ladies' room off the lobby to change her. The little squirt had made another mess, Steve thought fondly. He prowled the gift shop, keeping an eye peeled for Lynn, when a red-haired man drew his attention by erupting through the outer doors into the lobby. Hunched slightly, the man scurried toward the bank of elevators. He moved stiffly, despite his obvious haste, one hand pressed against the inside of his suit coat. His skin had a pasty, chalky look with two bright spots of color high on his cheekbones.

Steve couldn't say why he reacted as he did. Lots of men had red hair. The uneasy feeling that worked its way along Steve's scalp was something he couldn't ignore. He snatched the carrier and set off after the man at a trot.

Lynn came around the corner at that moment, the baby in her arms. Her eyes fastened on Steve. The red-haired man wasn't watching anything at all. They collided with a loud *oof.*

The man gave a grunt of pain as Lynn reeled backward. His freckled hand reached out as if to steady her and she lifted her head.

"You!"

The force of the word on his lips made it sound like an expletive. Steve was close enough to see the man's fingers tighten on Lynn's shoulders.

"Me?" She looked bewildered for just a moment and then astounded. "You're the man from the airport!"

"Give me the babe."

Steve had his semiautomatic in his hand, nearly concealed by the blanket trailing from the car seat. He thrust the nasty nose of the gun into Herbert's back. Instantly, the other man stilled.

"Don't move, Montgomery," Steve ordered.

The man uttered a low epithet, but he didn't move. He released Lynn, who stepped quickly away. Every muscle in Steve's body thrummed with tension, but the man continued to stand perfectly still.

"If you harm her, I'll see you both in hell," the man promised thickly.

"Hurt her? We were protecting her," Lynn said. "You're the one who nearly hurt her."

"Not here," Steve said. He moved the gun to jam it in the man's side. Their positions effectively blocked the weapon from the sight of anyone who might glance in their direction, but fortunately, the lobby was empty at the moment.

Steve applied enough pressure to indicate that he wanted Montgomery to turn and start walking. He didn't miss the indrawn hiss. There were brackets of pain around Montgomery's face. Something was wrong here.

"Lynn, grab Rachel's carrier. We're going to take Uncle Herbert here out to the car and have a little chat." She nodded once and reached for the car seat.

"How bad are you hurt?" Steve asked as they started toward the parking lot.

"I'll live to see you hang for kidnapping," the man snapped.

Steve felt a surge of admiration. "I hate to tell you, but we don't hang people over here anymore."

"Pity."

Steve grinned. "I think we need to talk."

"Ready to make your demands, are you? I can better whatever you're being paid, of course."

Steve sensed Lynn at his back. "No doubt. The car's over there."

"That's probably just as well," Herbert said weakly.

Steve frowned as he realized the man was at the end of his strength. He gestured, and Herbert opened the back door of the rental car. Lynn and the baby took the front passenger's seat. In the brief burst of yellow light from the overhead dome, Steve got a good look at Montgomery's face before the car door closed. It was pasty white, beads of sweat collecting on his forehead.

"Lynn, turn on the overhead light for a minute."

Before Montgomery could react, Steve peeled back the man's suit coat.

"Here now! What the bloody devil—"

"Damn."

"Oh, my God!"

The red stain covered most of what had once been a white shirt. The wound seeped slowly. Steve judged it had probably reopened only recently. A quick hand on the man's hot, dry cheek told the rest of the story.

"You damn fool, you're burning up. What was it? Gun, knife...?"

"Knife," he confirmed. "Crazy bitch."

Another piece clicked into place. "Alice?"

He heard Lynn's indrawn breath, but didn't look at her.

Herbert Montgomery leaned back against the seat and closed his eyes wearily. "I just wanted to help. Barrett was so afraid for Rachel, don't you see. He was terrified, really. It should have been a piece of cake, as they say, but there was no reasoning with the woman. I didn't mean to hurt her. She dashed her head." He shrugged and winced on a hiss of air.

And Steve did understand most of it. "You were trying to take the baby from Alice—"

"Actually, I went there to offer to buy Rachel." His lips clamped down on a low moan of pain.

"But Marcy took the baby, instead," Steve finished.

Herbert didn't respond. His eyes remained closed. Steve reached over and felt for a pulse. "Damn! Lynn. Go back inside. Tell them your husband found an unconscious man in the parking lot. Hurry."

Lynn threw open the door and ran back toward the brick building.

"Hang in there, Montgomery. Help's on the way." Steve replaced his gun, and pulled out a clean diaper. He folded back the man's shirt with care to reveal an angry, festering wound scabbed over in part, swollen, hot to the touch.

Herbert's eyes fluttered open. "Rachel," he muttered through dry cracked lips.

"She's right here. We'll get her back to Barrett," Steve promised. "Just take it easy."

Herbert started to say something, then closed his eyes again as though it was too much of an effort. Steve held the diaper over the wound until Lynn arrived with two paramedics and a security officer.

Herbert opened his eyes again once they got him on the gurney. His gaze wavered from Steve to the security man. "Couldn't make it inside, don't you know. They helped me," he forced out.

"Okay, buddy. Don't try to talk. Get him inside, Alan." The security man looked at Lynn, taking in her stricken expression, and at Steve who reached in the front seat to lift Rachel. "If you don't mind, I'll need your names and addresses for my report."

"Not at all," Steve agreed. "Come on, sweetheart."

"But—"

"The baby will be fine, honey. This won't take long, will it, Officer?"

Gratefully, the security man shot him a look of approval. "No, sir. Just a few quick questions for the report. Where did you find the man?"

"Over here by these bushes," Steve offered and described a fictitious scene. Lynn took Rachel from him and listened intently, throwing in an occasional corroboration the way she thought a real wife would. She expected the security man to comment on Steve's bruises, but he didn't. Maybe in the dark, he didn't even notice. He wrote down the fictitious name, address and phone number they gave him, thanked them and bade them good-night.

As they drove away several minutes later, Lynn tossed Steve an impish grin. "Will we go to jail for that—pretending to be some innocent couple?"

His lips twitched and he reached over to give her knee a quick squeeze. "Not a chance. You were fantastic."

"I was?"

"Absolutely."

She smiled and ducked her head at the compliment. "Thanks. Now, do you think you could explain what just happened back there? One minute, we have Herbert tagged as the bad guy, the next minute, he's an injured uncle trying to help his brother."

He pulled the car into the parking lot of their hotel. He turned off the ignition and twisted to face her. "Let's discuss it inside."

In their suite, Steve dropped the baby bag on the table and Lynn set the infant on the couch. Rachel was wide-awake and gurgled happily. Tiredly, Lynn flopped down beside her.

"Why aren't you sleepy?" she asked the baby.

"Maybe we should start drinking her formula."

Lynn made a face. "Have you smelled that stuff?"

"Yeah. That's probably what keeps her awake. How's Marcy doing?" he asked more seriously.

Lynn shut her eyes against the memory. "She's pretty confused. She rambled on about Alice and pills and the fire. It didn't make a whole lot of sense and that cough..."

His knuckle brushed her cheek and she leaned into the small caress.

"She'll be fine. The drugs probably keep her from sounding lucid. Don't forget, she's had a shock."

Lynn sighed. "I suppose. She really was confused. She even said Alice gave her the drugs."

"Kevin's drugs?"

Lynn's eyes closed, but her mind raced. "Must be, but it doesn't make sense."

He lifted her hand and encased it in his. "She'll be more coherent tomorrow. Why don't you use the bathroom first? I think we both need a good night's sleep tonight."

Sleep? He planned to sleep? She was exhausted, but much too wired for sleep.

"Your sister is safe," Steve went on. "The police are guarding Barrett Montgomery, and we have Rachel. In the morning, we'll turn ourselves in."

That stopped the flow of her other thoughts completely. "But what will happen to Rachel?"

"They'll put her in foster care until Barrett gets better."

"Oh, Steve, not foster care!"

Frustration was written on his expression, as well. "There isn't much choice. As soon as Herbert recovers, they'll probably name him as her guardian since he's her uncle. In the meantime, what else can they do?"

Steve felt an answering lurch of anguish as her eyes pleaded with him to prevent the baby from being taken from them. "We can't keep her, Lynn. You know that. I know how you feel, but they have special people who care for little babies like Rachel. She'll be fine."

He hated the look on Lynn's face as she stood and quickly exited the room. Rachel grabbed for the finger he held in her vicinity and he realized how much he, too, had bonded with the child. He hated the thought of her going into foster care, even temporarily. But what could they do?

"I suppose I could take a few more days off." Rachel gurgled happily. "Maybe Herbert could name us temporary guardians. That's if we don't end up in jail over this fiasco." Even as he said the words, he knew better. Given the current situation, no judge was going to award them custody of this baby.

He created a safe area for Rachel on the couch and headed into the bedroom for his new sweatpants. Lynn came out of the bathroom wearing the nightgown he'd bought her the other day. The sight stopped him midstep. What had ever made him think a long, shapeless garment with hundreds of tiny buttons up the front wasn't going to play havoc with his hormones?

It wasn't shapeless anymore. The soft folds of the material hugged her generous breasts and draped the rest of her lush figure in a way that made him want to start at the top button and work his way down, until he exposed every satiny inch of what lay underneath.

Lynn smiled seductively.

"All through? I need a shower," he managed to croak past the lump of desire lodged in his throat. He hoped she hadn't noticed the telltale bulge in his slacks. He was going to need a lengthy shower.

He was calm and in control when he emerged from the bathroom, toweling his hair and wearing only the dark sweatpants. The dim light by the bed was on, the outer room was dark. There was no sound from Rachel.

Lynn sat brushing her hair with slow, tantalizing strokes. "Rachel fell asleep."

The lace at her throat lent the white gown a virginal quality. She could have been a bride on her wedding night. A muscle he was very fond of jumped at that thought.

She looked up to meet his eyes. "Did you leave any hot water for the rest of the building?"

He couldn't tell her that at least part of his prolonged shower hadn't used any hot water at all. "I thought you'd be asleep by now."

"I was waiting for you."

He hated his immediate reaction to those softly spoken words. He told himself she didn't mean them the way they sounded. He told himself she could not help how beautiful she looked in the soft light of the room. He told himself he was going to have to go back in the bathroom and turn the cold tap on full for the next half hour, but his brain had snuck down to a lower portion of his anatomy and it wasn't the least bit interested in following this line of thought.

She placed the brush on the nightstand. "Which side of the bed do you prefer?"

Whichever side she was on.

"I don't think this is a good idea, Lynn." It took effort to get those lying words past his stubborn lips.

Her eyes traveled from his face to linger on his chest before moving to the bulge his sweatpants couldn't conceal.

"At least part of you thinks it's a wonderful idea."

Deliberately, she rose and threw back the sheet and blanket. She turned so the soft spill of light fell directly on her womanly shape.

While he watched, her fingers went to the top button of her gown. By the time she reached the third one, he had to clear his throat.

"Lynn, it's been a stressful couple of days. You don't want to do this."

Her eyes gleamed darkly. "I don't?"

The fourth button slid from its hole.

"No. I pushed you last night and we both know it."

Her fingers calmly released the next button.

"Funny, I remember a lot of stroking, but no pushing."

The sixth button gave way and the top of the gown parted slightly to reveal a breathtaking hint of creamy skin in the soft light. Steve couldn't take his eyes from Lynn's tapered fingers as they flowed slowly to the next button.

"You don't know what you're saying."

"Want to bet?"

The next button sprang free.

"Lynn, it's the heat of the moment. We've been through a lot the last few days." His body throbbed in denial. Why the hell was he arguing?

"Heat. Yes, I'm warm, all right."

The eighth button parted and she moved so the gown exposed quite a bit of one satiny mound.

She was teasing him. His prim and proper yuppie neighbor was a sultry tease. Her gaze returned to his pants and she smiled wickedly.

"One more button and I'm through being a nice, noble guy, Lynn," he warned.

The ninth button gave way. So did his patience.

The towel fell from his hands. With a groan, he slid his thumbs into the waistband of his pants. Her mouth parted and her fingers stilled as he inched them down past his navel. He was breathing heavily, but so was she. He stopped just short of revealing where the arrowing of fine hair from his navel was leading.

"Undo the next button."

Her eyes widened, then she smiled. Her fingers undid the next button.

"Pull it back, Lynn. It's only fair. You can see my chest. Let me see yours."

Her tongue darted out to moisten her lips and he thought he might lose control right there. "Ah, but you have hair covering your chest." Slowly, without looking away, she pulled aside both edges of the nightgown.

Steve took a deep breath to still the moan about to escape. They had just about pushed this game as far as it could go, he decided. Her breasts were gorgeous. Full and firm, the nipples puckered tightly, hard and pink and luscious.

"Your turn." She gave a toss of her head and several strands of hair fell forward over one eye.

In one fluid motion, he dropped the sweatpants and stepped out of them. He was rewarded by her sharply indrawn breath.

"Oh."

The tiny whisper of sound was all the more inflammatory.

"I think you had better finish removing that gown, Jerrilynn. I'm not sure I have enough restraint left to do the job properly."

Without a word, she released the gown from her fingers. It slid down her body to pool at her feet. She stood tall and proud before him, glorious in her nudity.

"C'mere," he said thickly. She came around the foot of the bed and into his arms, pressing against his body as though she could meld herself into him.

Steve rubbed their chests together in wicked stimulation. She arched her neck to expose the tender expanse of her throat and he set his mouth to taste and gently nip at the soft skin.

"Steve!"

"Did I hurt you?"

"No. Please kiss me."

He moaned or else she did. Their tongues entwined as his hands slid up her sides. She made a strangled sound as he slowly kneaded her flesh and bent to taste the point of one nipple.

Her fingers slid to him, squeezing gently. He knew he couldn't take much of that. He was too ready. Too needy. He brought one hand down to touch her intimately.

She moaned into his mouth. He backed her against the bed until she tumbled onto the sheets and he followed her down. He tested himself against her, but Lynn couldn't wait. She arched upward, hastening their union. Steve sank into her with a muffled cry.

Loving her was like nothing he had ever experienced before. She was incredibly responsive, wildly passionate. He felt the bite of her nails as her caresses became urgent, spurring him on. He swallowed her cry as she stiffened and arched in completion. Then he drove to his own fulfillment, uniting them in a burst of passion.

She gave a gentle moan of protest when he finally withdrew, her hands clutching his shoulders. He whispered her name as he reached for the blanket and sheet to cover them. She nestled against his chest with a sigh of contentment, her hair like spun silk against his bare shoulder. He had never felt so complete in his life.

Sometime in the night, Rachel woke them. Steve started to get up, but Lynn pushed him back. He waited patiently until she returned. This time, while the intensity of their lovemaking was the same, there was a tenderness that hadn't been possible the first time. The depth of his feelings stunned him. He fell asleep with Lynn in his arms once more, and his last thought was that he loved her.

RACHEL WAS HAVING a bad morning. She was fussy and generally irritable.

"She's just grumpy because of all the changes in her short life."

Lynn hoped he was right and prayed the baby wasn't coming down with anything. She liked playing mother, but she wasn't prepared to deal with a sick infant quite yet.

"Don't forget, we've been hauling her around like so much excess baggage for days now," Steve reminded her. "Heck, even I'm grumpy. I want more private time with you."

Lynn blushed at the heat in his eyes.

"Let her fuss a bit. It's the only way she can communicate right now."

He was right, she knew he was. But after he went out to phone Tim and pick up some breakfast, she found the baby's incessant cries setting her teeth together more firmly and more frequently than recommended by dentists and oral hygienists worldwide.

Rachel was giving her a headache.

"Come on, sweetheart, you're going to make yourself sick if you keep that up. You're also going to get us thrown out of here."

Lynn paced the floor, the screaming child on her shoulder, much too close to her ear. "Please, Rachel. Steve will be back soon. I know you like him better than me. I don't fault you, but you're too young for him, even if you did see him first."

She paused and turned on the television, hoping the noise would distract the baby or herself. Minutes later, she turned it off in disgust. Even Rachel seemed relieved. Not enough to stop crying, but at least she lowered her decibels a bit. Or maybe Lynn was finally, blissfully, going deaf.

"Okay, Rachel. I want him to hurry back, too. Steve's got a few rough edges, but that only makes him special. He likes babies. He'll make a terrific father."

Rachel's cries softened.

"You like the sound of my voice, huh? Okay, sweetie, then let me tell you the problem. He sees me as a yuppie. He thinks I'm committed to my work. Isn't that a laugh? I'd chuck it all for a chance to become part of his life. I love him."

Rachel's cries were definitely diminishing.

"I'd even be a help with his airpark. I do have a degree in business administration, you know." She thought for a second. "Do you think the parachuting bit is negotiable?"

"I'M GLAD you called," Tim told Steve. "Your favorite hospital was a very busy place last night."

"Marcy?"

"Montgomery."

Steve rubbed his jaw, wishing the baby had let them get just a little more sleep. Not that he would have missed a moment of his time with Lynn. "Herbert?"

"Wrong again. Barrett Montgomery. Someone dressed in an orderly's outfit tried to kill him again in the wee hours of the morning."

Stunned, Steve stared blankly across the street. "Could that someone have been Herbert?"

"Nope. Brother Herbert is firmly accounted for."

"Well, Kevin is dead, Lenny is gone, so who does that leave?"

"Unless you or Lynn are running around stabbing people, we're out of suspects," Tim told him.

"The police are going to love me."

"Hey, it's not that bad. There's a chance you and Lynn will only be mentioned as friends who've been baby-sitting for Barrett. Herbert can explain Alice's murder and tell them what he did with her body."

"Uh, Tim, what about the grocery store and the pizza parlor?"

"You broke no laws at the grocery store and we can finesse the pizza parlor incident. Weren't you simply yelling for a policeman to come and help?"

"You're devious."

"Thank you. It was Petey's suggestion."

"She's brilliant. Definitely, your better half." For a brief second, he pictured Lynn as his other half. "You're telling me we don't need a hotel room or a rental car anymore."

"Not unless you like spending money or think the person after Montgomery is apt to come after you."

"Not us. The baby."

"Let the cops do their job, Steve."

"You're right. I'll call you from jail."

"Don't worry, I make a great character witness."

Steve replaced the telephone and shoved his hand into his pocket. His fingers touched the wrinkled piece of paper. It probably wouldn't do any good, but he decided to call the clinic one more time. Lady Luck rode his shoulder. A different person answered the telephone and he asked for the doctor.

"One moment, sir."

"Matthew Abrams."

"Dr. Abrams, my name is Steven Gregory. I'm a licensed private investigator working out of the state of Maryland. Now, before you interrupt, I understand about patient confidentiality. I'm not asking for privileged information. In the course of an investigation I'm involved with, I came across a bill with your name and the name of Sunrise Clinic. The patient is listed as Mary A. Dunne."

Steve heard the small intake of breath.

"We have an infant baby girl whose mother has disappeared. We're trying to trace any other family the baby may have."

"What is the name of the child's mother?"

"Alice Dunne Montgomery. Mary may be a relative—"

"Describe Alice Dunne."

His suspicion became a certainty as the doctor confirmed his hunch. "I can't say for sure, of course, but I think Alice Dunne and Mary Alice Dunne are the same woman. Perhaps you could give me some details of your investigation?"

Sensing a concerned ally, Steve told him the story.

"I'm sorry to hear Mary may be dead. She was often delusional with what we call multiple personality disorder."

"I've heard of it. They've done movies."

"Yes, well," he harrumphed. "Mary was a very disturbed woman. Not dangerous, you understand. Or not to anyone other than herself, but then we never had enough time to delve into the complexities of her identities."

Steve thought about the picture of the happy couple on the beach. Was this why the Montgomerys were living apart? Not because Alice was in danger, but because she was insane?

"Mary has a long history with institutions such as ours," said the doctor. "She's been in and out of them since she was a teen."

Steve almost longed for a beard to tug on. He took several notes as the doctor talked, including the phone number for Mary's parents.

Alarm bells were clanging in the back of his head, but he wasn't sure why. After thanking the man and promising to call back, he phoned Lynn. Rachel's cries made the conversation difficult.

"The doctor was awfully forthcoming, considering he doesn't know anything about you, Steve."

"Mary Alice disappeared without a trace from his clinic three years ago. I think he's been troubled over that."

"She disappeared?"

A cold sort of numbness invaded his mind. The alarm bells were a thunderous din. "That's what he said."

"Steve?" He could hear the hesitation in her words. "What if she did it again? What if Alice isn't dead?"

The cold spread outward to invade every portion of his body. Rachel continued to cry as Lynn's voice took on a peculiar tone.

"You said follow the money. If Alice isn't dead, if Herbert didn't actually kill her, who stands to inherit with Barrett dead?"

Alice could be alive.

Lynn and Rachel were alone.

"I'll be right there. Don't open the door. Not for anyone!"

Steve dropped the receiver and raced for the car. Herbert never said Alice was dead. He said he didn't mean to hurt her.

A normal mother would be frantic to find her missing child—unless the mother was incapable—or insane. Someone stole Lynn's purse. One of the key cards to the hotel room had been inside. Jerrilynn was alone. He'd left her alone with the baby.

LYNN REPLACED the receiver and paced the room, the frantic baby on her shoulder. Fear clung to her like an ill-fitting cloak. There was no reason for the fear, she told herself. No one knew where she was, even if Mary Alice Dunne and Alice Montgomery were one and the same person.

Rachel hiccuped, and a key card was inserted in the door.

Lynn raised startled eyes. A stranger stood there, malice in every one of those set features.

"Bitch. The money's mine." Spittle accompanied the calm words. The woman's eyes were frosted in madness. The woman could only be one person.

Lynn turned and plunged into the bedroom, slamming the door closed. Without thought, she darted inside the bathroom and pushed the button lock.

Rachel began to scream in earnest. Her tiny wails echoed off the tile walls. There was nowhere to go.

They were trapped. The door handle rattled. Lynn laid the baby in the bathtub as Alice Montgomery hurled herself against the door. Would the door hold up under such a determined assault?

Frantically, Lynn searched for a weapon. There had to be something she could use. The woman was insane. The madness shone like a beacon from her demented eyes.

Maybe Lynn should get down. She could sit on the floor with her back against the door and brace her feet against the toilet bowl. Alice would expect her to be standing up. It might just give Lynn an edge.

The hammering and body lunges stopped abruptly before she could move. That was almost more terrifying. The silence was deafening. Even Rachel stopped crying.

Lynn's stomach clenched in fear. From outside the narrow door there was only silence. Was Alice baiting her? Trying to tempt her into unlocking the door? Was she waiting to pounce? Or had she left in frustration?

Lynn hated horror movies. More than anything, she hated the stupid characters who invariably opened a locked door, or stepped around a dark corner, knowing that something evil waited on the other side. But in that moment, Lynn suddenly understood the compulsion that prompted the fools to do just that. The waiting was unbearable.

What was Alice doing? Had she left? Was she hunting for something to batter down the door? Was she going for a gun?

Once again, Lynn searched the sterile room for anything she could use to defend herself and the baby. Towels, soap and tissue. Not even hair spray. Even the damn shower curtain rod was bolted into the wall.

Was that a noise?

Rachel resumed her cries as Lynn strained to hear. If Alice was still out there... She pressed her ear to the door.

Yes.

There was a definite rustling noise. Alice was still there. Dear God, where was Steve?

Alice was talking to herself, Lynn realized suddenly. It was a low, singsong voice. Lynn couldn't make out the words, but the bizarre tone was enough to strike a new chord of terror.

Alice sounded happy.

Lynn wanted to scream. Maybe she should. A scream might bring help. It also might bring death to anyone who answered her cry. The woman was mad.

Marcy's words echoed in her head. Marcy had said she'd gotten pills from Alice. Pills that made her sleepy. Lynn had thought she was confused. What if Marcy hadn't been confused? What if Marcy had been telling the truth? What if Marcy had been trying to tell her what had happened at the motel room?

What if Alice had tried to kill Lynn's sister as well as her own husband?

Lynn sniffed. And sniffed again. A tiny curl of smoke appeared under the door.

"Oh, my God!"

Alice had set something on fire.

Lynn panted in fear. Short gasps that fed off her terror. She and Rachel were really trapped. If she didn't open the door, there was no way out. If she did open the door, Alice would be waiting.

More smoke seeped under the crack. Her heart threatened to pound free of her chest. She heard a cackle of laughter.

"Think. Don't panic." The words reverberated over and over in her mind. She had to think. She had to stay calm. Otherwise, she would be dead.

Quickly, she grabbed a towel. Her fingers fumbled for the faucet and the cold water. She jammed the wet towel along the bottom of the door and wet another one. From outside, she heard another spate of laughter.

Eventually, the fire would trip the sprinklers and the alarm system. It would bring help on the run. But would it happen in time, or would she and Rachel be dead from smoke inhalation?

Anger surged through Lynn. She couldn't stay in here and let Rachel die. She had to do something. Even being shot or stabbed would be preferable to dying in the bathroom. If the woman had a gun, she would have used it by now. Herbert had been stabbed.

Lynn grabbed the bath mat and wound it around her left arm. She'd seen someone do that with a coat once in a movie. The trick was to deflect the knife with the arm that was covered, while using the other arm to subdue the person. Could she do that?

Oh, God.

Rachel sobbed steadily once more. Lynn wanted to join her. She spared the child a long glance. "I'll protect you, sweetie. Nothing's going to happen to you." She reached for the handle.

The door swung inward to reveal a blazing wastepaper basket. Alice lunged so fast, Lynn barely had time to deflect the arc of the knife with her protected arm.

Alice's eyes glowed with maniacal pleasure. There was no room to maneuver. Lynn realized at once she was no match for the woman. Her attention focused on the hand holding a large serrated knife. Suddenly, a strong, masculine hand enclosed Alice's wrist.

Alice screamed and twisted free in violent rage. Lynn recognized Steve, even as Alice launched herself at him with terrifying malevolence. Steve backed into the bedroom and Alice followed, slicing the air with the knife. Lynn spotted the comforter that lay mostly on the floor. Without pausing to think, she grabbed it. Just as Steve managed to wrench the knife from Alice's hand, Lynn threw part of the bulky comforter over the woman's head and grabbed her from behind.

Alice was like a wild thing. It took both of them to hold her as she thrashed against them. Without warning, the fire alarm cut loose with a raucous cry. In moments, they were soaking wet as the sprinkler system activated overhead.

In the end, the fire alarm brought help as well as an unexpected dousing. Since there was no sprinkler in the bathroom, only Rachel managed to stay dry.

At least outside her clothing.

"Are you okay?" Steve asked during a lull in the commotion around them.

Lynn soothed the crying child and nestled closer to the man at her side. It took two officers to carry the manacled, still-struggling Alice from the room.

"I am now."

"I love you."

Her eyes blinked back a sudden sheen of tears. "Well, thank God. I was afraid I was going to have to try and make partner in my firm, after all."

He studied her, and then his dimples appeared. "You already made partner. You're my partner, from now on."

Epilogue

A silent scream climbed her throat. As she watched, he drew back a powerful arm and the hammer delivered a smashing blow to the obstinate nail. A segment of wood splintered and flew from the board to plunge unseen to the dirt below.

He leaned back ever so slightly to peer upward. The entire length of the rickety wooden ladder swayed and shuddered perilously.

"Damn. I think I killed it."

From somewhere, she found the ability to speak quietly. "What do you think you're doing?"

Again, the ladder wavered as he reacted to the sound of her voice. Sheepishly, he looked down.

"Oh. You're back. I didn't hear the car. How's Marcy?" He twisted and the ladder creaked and wobbled.

"Almost her old self again. She really likes living in the halfway house. What are you doing?"

"That big nail worked itself loose again. We're going to have to replace the entire sign."

Lynn glared at the sturdy man on the flimsy wooden ladder that was older than her grandmother. "Come down from there."

"Okay, but the ladder is perfectly safe." The ladder protested as he shifted positions. "Social Services called right after you left. Rachel's thriving. They've placed her with a great family until Barrett gets out of the hospital."

"Why doesn't Herbert take her when he's released?"

"His visa's about to expire, and they won't let him take Rachel out of the country."

He tossed aside the hammer, which landed with a thud in the grass several yards to the left. Then he smiled. She could see the dimples that bracketed his firm mouth.

"I also learned they're moving Alice to a state institution tomorrow." There was an ominous creak as he started to descend. "Uh, could you hold the ladder for me?"

"That isn't a ladder. It's kindling." But she hurried forward as his foot searched for the next rung.

"Don't be silly. It's perfectly serviceable."

"As kindling," she affirmed.

"That's ridiculous. It's old, but it's sound."

He was more than halfway down when the rung cracked under his weight. She heard him say something, but the actual words were lost when everything happened at once.

The rung gave way. Steve let go of the ladder and leapt to one side as the wood was torn from Lynn's grip. For a moment, neither of them spoke. Her words were accompanied by a decided quiver, but were eloquent nonetheless. "You idiot! You could have been killed!"

Before she could take three steps in his direction, he was there, his warm strong arms enfolding her. His gentle lips placed butterfly kisses in her hair, on her face, on her...

"Stop it right there, buster."

"You don't like that?"

"No."

"Liar."

"Fool."

"I'm sorry." He met her eyes with tender concern.

"You should be." She wasn't willing to let him off quite that easily. "What if you had fallen? You could have broken your neck, and I'd be stuck with an airpark I don't know how to run and a baby with no father."

He went motionless.

"Baby?"

"I'm not even certified to fly yet, let alone teach someone else. I'd have to hire more people and I'd probably go broke and the baby and I would starve—"

He grabbed her by the shoulders and captured her stormy gray eyes with his own. "Are you telling me we're going to have a baby?"

The gray softened to that feathery shade he loved so much. "Why are you so surprised? You did help with the project, you know."

He held her then. Fiercely, tenderly, exultantly. Words wouldn't make it past the lump in his throat. He closed his eyes for a moment and then opened them.

"This time, it won't be somebody else's baby," she told him with love in her eyes. "This time, it will be our baby."